Helplessly trapped in the middle of pimp wars and drug trafficking, Kari Allensworth knew that death lurked around every corner and there was no escape from her life as a street-walker. But one night she was presented with a book in which she read about another abused prostitute whose life was saved by the love of Jesus Christ. Could He deliver Kari from her hardened, violent life-style? *Kari* will make a far-reaching impact on your life as it proves that with Christ nothing is impossible.

These books may be purchased from Christian bookstores, book racks, or directly from John Benton Books. You may write to John Benton Books for a book order form:

JOHN BENTON BOOKS
BOX 94304
218 SO. MADISON
PASADENA, CA 91109

CARMEN   SANDI
JULIE   AUGIE
DEBBIE   KARI
LEFTY   TRACY
VICKIE   PACO
JACKIE   KRISTI
TERRI   LORENE
NIKKI   ROCKY
CONNIE   RENEE
VALERIE   LISA
SHELIA   PATTI
DENISE   SHERRIE
STEPHANIE   LORI
CANDI
DO YOU KNOW WHERE YOUR CHILDREN ARE?

Kari

John Benton

John Benton Books
Box 94304
218 So. Madison
Pasadena, CA 91109

ISBN: 0-8007-8491-X

Kari

1

It was easy to tell when my mother came home. When she walked up the front steps, she was either singing or cursing—and always drunk.

I was sitting in the front room, watching TV, when I heard Mom. She was laughing and singing this time.

The door burst open. There stood Mom. "Kari, darling. Look what I've got for you."

Sometimes, out of guilt, Mom would buy me a present. It could be anything from an almond-loaded candy bar to a new pair of jeans.

As soon as she said that, I jumped up and started toward the door. But then I stopped. Standing behind Mom was a huge man. He had a big grin on his face.

"Kari, I brought home a friend." Mom looked at the man, then back at me, and said, "This is Lawrence Alban, Kari."

Mr. Alban and I stared at each other. His eyes widened as he looked me up and down. That made me uncomfortable.

"At least shake hands with Lawrence," Mom said.

I started backing up. This Alban guy looked like a real creep. I didn't like the look in his eyes, especially when they started examining my body. I had an idea he was up to no good.

Before I could say anything, the big guy started toward me. Then he lunged at me and threw his huge arms around me. The first thing that hit me was his breath. He was stinking drunk.

Then he pulled me close. I glanced over at Mom. She was laughing. Mr. Alban squeezed harder. He pressed his body fully against mine. I felt dirty and degraded. I struggled.

Then I felt his hand on my back. It started feeling around, lower and lower. That's when I jerked my knee up real fast. The guy jumped back and doubled over. "That'll teach you," I snarled.

"Kari, you little brat," Mom hollered. "How dare you do that!"

I pointed at her groaning friend. "The next time you bring a guy home, teach him to keep his filthy hands in his pockets," I flared.

"Now, Kari, Mr. Alban didn't mean any harm. He's a wonderful man. You know, he's got three children of his own."

"Well, what's he doing here, then?" I countered. "Don't you think he ought to go home to his wife and kids?"

Mr. Alban struggled upright and wagged a finger at me. "Listen here, little girl. I should take you over my knee and spank you good. That's what you need."

"Mister, that'll be the last little girl you spank," I

sneered. "You lay your hands on me again, and I'll kill you!"

"Kari, you shut your mouth, you hear me?" Mom started toward me. Suddenly she tripped and fell flat on her face. She tried to get up, but she was too drunk.

Lawrence reached down and tried to pick her up. He was staggering, too. While he was bent over, I felt like giving him a good, hard kick right where it hurts.

The two finally made it to their feet. "I think you should go to your room," Mom told me.

Mr. Alban leered at Mom. I knew what he had on his mind.

Mom's drinking was going to be the end of her. She kept getting worse and worse. In the three years since Dad had died, I'd never known Mom to have a sober day. And worse, it seemed as though men kept taking advantage of her. I shook my head as I headed for my room.

"You certainly are a cute little thing, Kari," Mr. Alban called after me.

I stopped and spun around. "I may be five foot two and a hundred and five pounds, and the boys might think I'm attractive, but I want to tell you something, Mr. Alban, another smart remark like that, and I'll scratch your eyes out!"

He laughed. I started toward him. I was so mad right then, I was trembling.

Then Mom stepped between us. She grabbed me by the shoulders and shook me. "Honey, don't you dare lay a hand on Lawrence. He and I have plans."

"You have what?"

"Well, we plan to get married tomorrow. Reverend Ashley has agreed to marry us, and you're invited to our wedding."

"What?" I yelled. "You're going to marry this stinking bum?"

"Yes, honey. I'm in love with Lawrence."

"Mom, let's talk about this. Why didn't you discuss it with me? How long have you known him? How do you know he'll make a good husband? He's not going to live in this house with us, is he?"

Mom grabbed me by the arm and led me down the hall. Mr. Alban plopped down in the big chair and stared at the TV.

When we got to my bedroom, Mom opened the door and pushed me in. "Kari, I wanted to talk to you, but I was just afraid to," she started. "I mean, I've been so lonely, honey. I need a man around the house."

"Mom, I think you're making a mistake," I said. "It's been tough since Dad died, but don't take just any man that comes down the road. That guy is no good!"

"Don't say that, honey. I've known him for a while now, and he's a very nice man."

"What do you mean, you've known him for a while? How long have you known him?"

"Let's just say for quite some time," Mom said.

"This is the first time I've heard anything about this Lawrence Alban," I persisted. "You never talked to me about him before. Tell me, exactly how long have you known him?"

Mom stared at the floor. "One week," she admitted.

That did it. "I can't believe this!" I exploded. "All the times you lectured me about my boyfriends. I'm sixteen years old, and I make mistakes once in a while. But you're forty, Mom. You should know better. Can't you see that guy's bad news?"

"Honey, don't say that. I'm sick and tired of being lonely."

"Mom, I want to tell you something about him," I said urgently. "When he first looked at me, I got a real strange feeling. That man is on the make. I mean, he's no good! I wouldn't trust him one bit. He's a dirty old man with filthy, dirty things on his mind."

Mom just stood there, staring at the floor. She finally looked up at me. "You can say all you want to, Kari. I've already made up my mind. He's mine, and I'm not going to lose him."

Mom walked out of the room and slammed the door. I heard her footsteps going back down the hall.

How could Mom be so stupid? I thought. Why couldn't she see through that guy?

I stayed in my bedroom the rest of the evening. I tried to study, but couldn't concentrate. I kept thinking about Dad. I wished he were still alive.

Every once in a while, I would hear Mom and Lawrence giggling. I really wanted to go out there and tell that jerk to leave my mother alone, but he and Mom were both drunk and probably wouldn't remember what I'd say anyway.

They were still carrying on when I got into bed. I never did hear Mr. Alban leave.

When I got up the next morning, Mom wasn't up yet. Her bedroom was just down the hall. I tiptoed to her room, slowly turned the knob, and gently opened the door. I looked across the room to Mom's bed. There she lay, sound asleep. Then I gasped. Lying next to her was Mr. Alban.

My first impulse was to run in and jerk him out of bed, but I held myself back.

Why would Mom do this to me? At least she could have waited until they were married. I closed the door and went to make myself some breakfast before going to school.

It was hard to concentrate in class that day. At least I was a senior, and this was my last year. I was going to move out of the house as soon as I graduated.

When I got home that afternoon, no one was around. I knew what was happening. Mom had said she was getting married, and I knew she wouldn't back out.

Mom still wasn't home at supper time. If she was going on a honeymoon, why hadn't she told me?

I finally fixed my own supper. I kept waiting for Mom to come home.

Later that evening I heard her coming, singing and laughing, but I also heard another voice singing and laughing. I knew who that was—Mr. Alban.

Mom came through the front door. She had a

pretty dress on. Mr. Alban had on a suit. As soon as Mom saw me, she yelled, "Welcome your daddy home."

That was too much for me. I jumped up and ran to my bedroom. I felt like vomiting.

After I slammed my bedroom door, I threw myself across the bed and started crying. Why did this have to happen to me?

I kept thinking about my real dad. If he could just come back somehow. I loved him so much, and I knew he'd understand and take me out of this mess. But I knew that it would never happen. He was dead and gone forever.

The next few days were tough. Mr. Alban had no job. Mom was living on her Social Security and part of Dad's insurance. And they were drinking right in the house.

Mr. Alban should find a job, I thought. At least he would be out of the house some of the time. But he didn't seem to worry about that.

And he kept staring at my body. I wanted to scratch the eyeballs right out of his head. I don't mind people looking at me, but I resent it when they drop their eyes and start staring at certain parts of my body.

A couple of times I told Mom about it. She just laughed. The last time I mentioned it she said, "Oh, he's just sexy."

Mom refused to believe me. As far as I was concerned, the guy was a dirty old man.

Then it happened about a month later. Mr. Alban

made arrangements for Mom to go to an A.A. meeting. He said he could quit drinking on his own, but Mom needed help.

That evening Mr. Alban and I were alone. I was scared to death, so I stayed in my bedroom.

I was lying on the bed, studying algebra, when my bedroom door opened. There stood Mr. Alban, grinning at me.

Before I could move, he was tearing at my clothes. I did my best to fight him off, but it didn't help. He was too big and strong. It was all over in a few minutes.

When he was done, Mr. Alban got up and walked to the door. Then he turned around and looked at me. "You'll get over it, Kari. Everything's going to be okay."

I just stared at him. I think I was in shock. I felt numb, and I knew I was going to vomit.

He pointed his finger at me. "If you dare tell anybody what happened, I'm going to kill you. I'm not afraid to kill you. Do you understand what I'm saying?"

My heart was beating like crazy. I was literally scared out of my wits. I stared at him, and he stared right back.

He started toward me. I couldn't move, I was so terrified.

He pointed at me again. "Do you understand what I'm saying, young lady? If you dare breathe a word to anybody, I'm going to kill you."

That's when I shook my head. "I'll never say anything," I quavered.

He was still pointing his finger at me. "You'll get over this."

But I knew I never would. I felt so filthy, dirty, and ashamed. I felt dirtier than a sewer.

Mr. Alban walked out and shut the door. I lay there, staring straight up at the ceiling. What should I do now? Should I call the police? But I knew he'd kill me if I tried.

I don't know how long I lay there. The next thing I remember, Mom was at my door. I turned and stared at her.

"Kari, I have some great news for you," she said.

"What news is that?" I asked, trying to make my voice sound normal.

Mom came over to the bed, reached down, and hugged me. "I've stopped drinking."

"That's nice," I mumbled.

"Honey, you don't sound excited. I was at A.A. tonight, and I heard people who used to have terrible drinking habits. They're free now, and I'm going to be just like them. I'm going to be free, too!"

I tried to sound excited. "That's great, Mom, just great."

Mom looked at me. "Kari, is something the matter?" she asked.

I had better think of something to tell her. "I think I've got the flu," I said. Then it hit me. I felt my stomach turn. There was no way I could stop it. I rolled over and was sick right then.

Mom said, "Oh, honey, you're sick, poor thing."
If Mom only knew.

"Lawrence, Lawrence! Come here quick," Mom
yelled.

"Don't call him," I pleaded, but it was too late. My
bedroom door flew open. There stood Mr. Alban.
Just the sight of him made me cringe.

"What happened?" he asked.

"Kari's got the flu and just got sick all over the
floor," Mom told him. "Quick, go get the mop."

Much to my surprise, Mr. Alban turned and left.
Then he came back with the mop.

He started mopping the floor near my bed. I
couldn't even look at him. I turned and faced the
wall.

I wanted to scream that Mr. Alban had raped me,
but somehow I just couldn't get it out. Maybe it was
best. He would probably go get a butcher knife and
kill me right there.

That night I didn't sleep at all. And I didn't feel
like going to school the next day.

Mom came in the next morning to see how I was
doing. I looked up at her. She was shaking. "What's
the matter?" I asked.

"I need a drink, honey, but I'm not going to take
one. I'm just not going to take a drink. I want to make
it through this. I just called my counselor, and she
talked me through it. I want to make it."

It would never happen, I knew. Many times Mom
had told me she'd never drink again, but she always
did.

That afternoon Mom brought me some soup. I noticed she wasn't shaking anymore.

When she bent over me, I smelled her breath. She'd hit the bottle again.

"It's tough, isn't it, Mom?" I said gently.

She didn't say a word, but just looked down into my face. Then I saw the big tears. They started rolling down her cheeks.

"Mom, someday you're going to lick the problem," I told her. "I know you will. You can do it, Mom."

"Honey, isn't there any way out of this for me? I just wish I was different. I wish I would never, never drink again. But I just can't help myself. I can't help myself."

Mom started to sob. I reached up and drew her head down next to mine.

She smelled like a liquor store, but she still was my mother, and I loved her. We'd gone through a lot together after Dad died. I brought her close to me and hugged her tight.

"Mom, everything is going to be okay," I soothed. Mom kept sobbing. I tried my best to comfort her, but I knew my words weren't very convincing. I knew everything was not going to be okay.

Mom finally got up and left the room. I ate the soup. I felt a little bit better, though I still hurt from that vicious beast. And I knew one thing. I would never, never in my life, forgive him for that. Someday I was going to get even.

I stayed in bed all that day. A couple of times when

I got up to go to the bathroom, I could hardly walk. The pain was excruciating.

Mr. Alban was gone somewhere the whole day. I was glad I didn't have to face him.

Mom brought some supper to me in my room. She was a lot worse off than she had been in the morning.

"Mom, why don't you go back to A.A.," I suggested. "I know they've helped some people."

"It won't work for me, honey," she answered. "There must be another way."

As soon as I mentioned A.A., I realized it had been a stupid suggestion. I never wanted to be alone with Mr. Alban again. If Mom ever left the house, I was going to leave at the same time.

"Are you feeling better?" Mom changed the subject.

"Mom, do you know why I'm sick?" I asked.

Mom jerked back. "Are you pregnant, Kari?"

"I hope not," I told her.

"What do you mean, you hope not?" she gasped. "Have you been doing things you shouldn't?" I turned and looked the other way. Mom reached over and grabbed me. "Honey, if you're pregnant, you'd better get an abortion. I don't want you to be a disgrace to Lawrence and me."

That did it. "Mom, if you only knew," I blurted.

"What do you mean?" she demanded. "You tell me right now. Are you pregnant?"

"Mom, I don't know if I'm pregnant," I snapped.

"Listen, young lady, don't you get smart with me. What have you been doing?"

Should I tell Mom the truth? Would she believe me?

I took a deep breath. I was going to tell her anyway. Even if Mr. Alban killed me.

2

My heart was beating like crazy. Would Mom believe me? I had to go ahead with it. "Mom, I've got something to tell you."

Mom looked at me expectantly. I wondered how she would react to what I had to say.

"Yes, honey, what is it?"

"Mom, Mr. Alban raped me."

Mom didn't bat an eyelid. She just turned and started for the bedroom door. I reached up and grabbed her arm. "Didn't you hear what I said? I said that dirty, filthy, good-for-nothing bum you call your husband raped me!"

Mom started to pull away. I jerked on her arm as hard as I could. "Mom, didn't you hear me?"

"Oh, Kari, I used that excuse when I was a teenager. One time my boyfriend and I were fooling around in the backseat of his car. So I made up a big story. To this day, my parents think I was raped. So don't try that one on me."

"Mom, you've got to believe me," I pleaded. "It happened last night while you were at the A.A. meeting. He came into my room and raped me. I'm telling you, Mom, I'm not lying!"

My voice was getting higher. Mom laughed. "So help me, Kari, you're saying exactly what I said. In fact, I ripped my clothes and rubbed some dirt on myself. Then I bawled like a baby. My mom and dad went for it. So don't try to pull that one on me."

"I wasn't sick with the flu," I insisted. "Mr. Alban did rape me last night. It's the truth, Mom."

Mom got up and started to walk away. "Well, I'll talk to Lawrence about this," she told me. "I know he didn't rape you, young lady. That's a vicious lie. And furthermore, if I were you, I'd go see the doctor. And I'd tell whoever got you pregnant, that he'd better stop fooling around like that, or the police will hear about it." Mom stalked out of my bedroom and down the hall.

A little later I heard Mr. Alban come in. He was laughing and giggling. I knew what that meant. He was drunk.

Soon after I heard him yell, "Why, that little devil! She's a dirty liar."

I knew what had happened. Mom had told him. There was only one thought on my mind. Mr. Alban was going to kill me now.

They both came stomping down the hall to my bedroom. The door burst open. Mr. Alban came in, with Mom trailing behind. He stood right over my bed and glared at me. "What's this story your mom told me? You're accusing me of rape, young lady?"

I slid across the bed and braced my back against the wall. If he lunged at me, I planned on doing my best to defend myself.

"I want to tell you something," Mr. Alban ranted. "I had a daughter just like you, and she accused me of the same thing. I got into big trouble!"

Mr. Alban's eyes were ablaze with anger. I couldn't believe he could tell these lies with a straight face.

"Mom, don't you believe him," I said. "This man is a rapist and a liar!" I pointed right at him.

Mr. Alban grabbed my arm and jerked me across the bed. His hand came down hard against my face. The force of the blow sent me sprawling across my bedroom.

My jaw hurt like crazy. I'd better be careful. I knew I couldn't take too many more hits like that.

He ran over and stood over me. He started cursing, then he continued, "That daughter of mine went to the police, and they came and took me away."

I looked over at Mom. She was glaring down at me. I knew she didn't believe me. I was dealing not only with a maniac, but a professional liar as well.

"My daughter finally admitted she had lied," Mr. Alban said. He was calming down a little now. "But the damage was already done. I lost my job, and I was an outcast in my own community. My daughter finally confessed, but it was too late." I stared at Mom. She was hanging on every word Mr. Alban said. "Oh, Lawrence, how terrible, how terrible," she said. "You never told me that."

I was mad and disgusted and sick, but I didn't want to say one word. I had to figure out what to do now. I knew Mr. Alban was going to get me later.

He finally backed off. Mom walked out of the room first, but Mr. Alban stood there glaring at me. Then he bent down and whispered, "You didn't believe me, did you, Kari? Just wait until we're alone again." He rubbed his hands together in anticipation.

"You filthy liar," I yelled.

He doubled up his fist. I covered my head, but this time he hit me square in the stomach. The pain was excruciating. I bent over and tried to get my breath back.

When I looked up, there was Mom standing in the doorway. "What happened?" she asked.

"She's just admitted she's been lying," Mr. Alban told her, "so I had to slap her. I just barely touched her, and she acts as if she's dying. This daughter of yours is nothing but filth, and I mean filth. She's probably full of VD, too."

I gritted my teeth. Although I was lying on the floor, I wanted to kick and scream and gouge Mr. Alban's eyes out. But he was too big for me.

"Well, you two will probably get along eventually," Mom shrugged. "At least I hope so."

I can't describe the hatred I felt in my heart toward that beast that was still standing over me. If I ever got the chance, someday I would get even with him.

They walked out of the room. I crawled over and lay on my bed. I knew a man that violent was capable of murder. I had to get out, and quick.

I waited until Mom and the beast went to bed.
Then I started packing. I felt like writing a note, but I
decided against it. Mom wouldn't believe me anyway.

Finally I picked up my suitcase and slipped out my
bedroom window. As soon as I got down on the
street, I had a strange feeling. I felt free.

My first thought was where I could go. I knew I'd
have to get far away. I wondered how a New Jersey
girl like me would do in Florida. It seemed as though
everybody that ran away from home ended up on the
beach in Fort Lauderdale. I'd fool them all and head
for California, I decided.

When I got to the corner, I stuck out my thumb. A
guy picked me up. Hitchhiking turned out to be much
easier than I had thought. It seemed as though guys
wanted to pick up girls. I was cautious, though. I kept
telling different stories.

One story I told was that I was on my way to col-
lege and needed to save money because tuition was so
high. Some guys swallowed that.

Other times I told them I was going out to see my
mom in California. I told them I couldn't stand living
with my dad. Some guys even gave me money for my
trip.

By the time I landed in Los Angeles five days later,
I had accumulated twenty dollars. I headed toward
Sunset Strip in Hollywood, one of the places I'd
heard about.

The sun was warm on the Strip—and this was
March. I thought about the weather back in Jersey. It
was cold and damp there, but here it was nice.

What should I do now? Where should I stay? I hadn't the slightest idea.

I needed to take a shower and change my clothes. I hadn't stopped overnight on my trip, just slept in cars as I came across the country.

As I stood there, wondering what to do, a girl walked up. She smiled at me, but I knew something was up. "Hi, what's your name?" she asked.

Better give a false name, I decided. "My name is Marilyn Johnson," I told her.

The girl laughed. "Hey, babe, like what's your real name?" She seemed awfully nosy. Was she trying to make conversation, or what? I stood there, staring at her. Maybe she was a religious nut. I had heard there was a bunch of those people in California.

I had to get rid of her. "I'm just waiting for my dad to come and pick me up," I improvised. "He's a member of the L.A. Police Department."

She giggled again. "You mean a cute little girl like you is going to spend the weekend in the mountains with your father? Don't you know you can get arrested for that? I mean, who would believe that story?"

Whatever this girl was, she was smart. But who was she, anyway? I might as well find out. "Are you a prostitute?" I asked suspiciously.

"No, come on. You must think better of me than that."

"Sure you are," I insisted. I'd never really met a prostitute before, so I wasn't sure. This girl was nicely dressed, but I had heard that Sunset Strip wasn't a very good place. I had seen it in a couple of movies. There were prostitutes around there.

"Listen, I live just up the block," she said. "I have the day off, but I'm a secretary at Universal Studios. I just noticed you looked kind of lonely, and I thought I'd make conversation. Is that okay with you?"

I felt like an idiot. Here I had accused this poor girl of being a prostitute! "Okay, I'll level with you," I said. "I just ran away from home in New Jersey, and my dad's not a cop."

She stepped up to me and put her arm around me. "Listen, a lot of runaways land here on Sunset Strip. I've lived here for five years now. A lot of homeless kids are really mixed up, and I've been able to spot them now and then. As soon as I saw you, I knew you were a runaway."

"I'm really in a jam," I confessed. "I don't even have a place to stay."

She giggled again. I was enjoying her giggle by now. It sounded nice and cheerful.

"Well, I have this friend who's picking me up," she told me. "Would you like to go for a ride and see some of the sights?"

I still couldn't break through the fear barrier. Something seemed wrong. "With who? Your pimp?" I blurted out.

She laughed. "Oh, come on. I thought we went over that. My boyfriend's a very nice guy. He's a successful businessman."

That made me feel a little better. At least he was a businessman. I was going to keep my eyes open, though.

Just then a car pulled up. It was a gorgeous Rolls Royce, absolutely spotless.

"This is my successful boyfriend," the girl told me. "I have good taste, huh?"

I'd never, ever ridden in a Rolls Royce before. I wondered what kind of business this guy was in. He got out of the car and walked over to us.

"Beatrice, who's that with you?" he asked casually. I looked at him. He was dressed impeccably, and he had two gold chains around his neck. I looked at his wrist—more gold. Then I saw some big diamonds on his fingers. That made me nervous. He looked like a pimp.

The girl said, "Paco, this is my new friend from New Jersey. I told her you and I were going sight-seeing and invited her along. Is that okay with you?"

My heart started beating faster. Who was this guy, anyway? Was he really a pimp?

Paco walked over to me and stuck out his hand. I expected him to grab me and stuff me into the trunk of his car.

I gave him my hand. He took it in both of his and patted it. "Listen, young lady. This is probably not the best place for you to be. It's dangerous here in the street."

Paco seemed to be really concerned about me. I felt better about him already.

"Oh, I forgot to introduce myself," Beatrice said.

"I'm Beatrice Merrell, and this is Paco, my friend. He's a very wealthy businessman."

Beatrice and Paco both laughed. Were they kidding?

"My name is Kari Allensworth," I told them.

Paco reached for the car door. "Come on, Kari. Let's get you out of this place. There are some wonderful sights to see in Los Angeles."

"I was telling Kari that I work at Universal Studios," Beatrice said. "Maybe we could go by and meet my boss."

This wasn't so bad after all. Here I was going to see Hollywood. And I had heard about Universal Studios. They have tours, and you can see the shark from *Jaws*.

Paco opened the front door for me. I stepped in and sat down. I have never felt such luxury in all my life. It must be a dream, I thought. I was sitting in a Rolls Royce!

Beatrice got in the backseat. Paco walked around and got in on the other side. We started off. I still couldn't believe this car.

We went a couple of blocks down the Strip. Paco slowed down and pulled over to the curb.

"Kari, I want you to take a look at someone," he said. "I must warn you, this is probably the most dangerous man in the world." Paco was pointing across the street. I saw a well-dressed guy standing there.

"That guy's name is Ripper," Paco told me. I glanced back at Beatrice, and then at Paco. Beatrice said, "He's called Ripper because of his right hand.

Take a look at his right hand. Can you see it?"

I kind of squinted my eyes. Then I saw it. The man had a huge hook sticking out of his sleeve.

"The poor guy only has one arm, huh?" I asked.

"First of all, he's not a poor guy," Paco said. "The reason he's called Ripper is that hook on his arm is filed sharp as a razor blade. He's been known to rip people apart. He is vicious!"

"Well, why don't the cops come and put him away?" I wanted to know. "You mean they let murderers run loose on the streets?"

Beatrice said, "He's a pimp. That's what Paco is trying to tell you. A vicious pimp. Don't ever talk to him. If he comes around, start running."

I was scared. And then it hit me. Why would these people tell me all this? Something wasn't quite right here.

We drove a couple more blocks. Paco pulled over to the curb again and said, "Here's another guy you have to look out for. This guy has about six girls working for him, and every once in a while one of the girls comes up missing. The rumor is that he takes them to the mountains in Nevada and kills them, then buries them there. Don't ever go to work for that guy. It could cost you your life."

I looked at Paco's hands again. Two diamonds on each hand. He must be a pimp! I said, "Okay, you two, why are you telling me about this? How come you know these pimps?"

Paco laughed. "I've been around, baby. I've been around."

Beatrice explained. "Paco owns a Rolls Royce dealership. He sells Rolls Royces to a lot of Hollywood
stars, but he also sells them to the pimps. He really
doesn't like to do business with pimps, but they always pay in cash."

"Is that what you really do?" I asked.

Paco nodded. "Yep, that's my business. As far as
I'm concerned, they ought to take those pimps to the
hills of Nevada and bury them alive."

That made me feel better. I started to breathe a little easier. I figured I could trust Beatrice and Paco.

We drove through some beautiful suburbs. Then
we drove on some kind of expressway.

"Can't we visit Universal Studios?" I asked.

"Well, maybe we could just drive by," Beatrice said
hesitantly. "I don't know if I should go in to my office. You see, on my day off they really don't like me
coming around. My boss has this funny thing about
your day off. He doesn't want to see you at the
office."

Paco pointed out a sign to me. "There's Universal
Studios, Kari. Maybe when Beatrice is working you
could go on the tour. It's a fantastic thing."

"Listen, why don't we go in there now?" I suggested. "I've heard so much about it. We've got time,
don't we? I mean, nothing's really happening today,
is it?"

Beatrice and Paco exchanged looks. Then Beatrice
said, "Why don't we drive over to Malibu. You've
heard about Malibu, haven't you?"

The name sounded familiar, but I didn't know

much about it. "Is that part of Hollywood?" I asked.

"Well, I guess maybe you could call Malibu part of it," Paco said. "That's where the movie stars live. They live right on the ocean." That sounded rather exciting. We got on the freeway and headed in that direction.

We drove along the coast. It was absolutely beautiful. I just couldn't get over riding in that Rolls Royce. People kept staring at us, and I felt so important.

When we got to Malibu, it wasn't what I had expected. The houses were so close together. Paco pointed out the stars' homes to me. I had thought movie stars lived in huge houses.

"Back East they told us Hollywood stars lived in mansions," I said. "These don't look like mansions to me."

Beatrice laughed. "You're talking about Beverly Hills, Kari. Some movie stars live there. In fact, that's where Paco lives."

"Are you kidding?" I said. "You live in a mansion?"

"Yep," Paco said. "I have a gorgeous place."

We turned back toward Hollywood. It didn't take us long to get to a beautiful residential area.

We drove by some homes. It was everything I'd heard about it—all gorgeous mansions.

Then we turned into a driveway. There were gates. I noticed Paco reach under his seat and push something. The gates opened automatically.

We drove up a long driveway and then to the main house. I couldn't believe it. It was a magnificent mansion. There were huge palm trees and beautiful flowers and such green grass.

"Paco, is this really yours?" I breathed.

He smiled. "Yep, babe. All mine."

We pulled up in front of the mansion. I got out. I noticed Beatrice grab my suitcase. Were they really going to let me stay here overnight?

Just then a man dressed as a butler came and took my suitcase. That made me a little bit nervous. Was I a guest or a prisoner? What if Paco was a pimp after all?

We walked through the front door. There was a long hallway. A girl hurried by me. When I looked at her face, I gasped. It was black and blue. I had heard about pimps beating up their women.

I stopped and turned to Paco and Beatrice. "What happened to that girl?"

Paco said, "I found her last night out in the street. Some pimp beat her up."

I suppose I should have felt relieved, but I didn't. I was scared. I didn't believe Paco.

3

"Why don't you stay here overnight?" Beatrice suggested, after Paco had excused himself for a few minutes.

"Well, things feel a little bit different around here," I stammered. "It's a beautiful place and everything, but I think maybe I'd better be going."

Beatrice grabbed my arm. "Hey, don't be afraid. I know how you feel." I stared at Beatrice. How could she know what I was feeling?

"Five years ago I ran away from San Francisco," Beatrice explained. "I ended up on Sunset Strip. I can't tell you how afraid I was. I mean, I just knew I was going to get raped and killed! And besides all that, I was hungry. I hadn't eaten for two days, but I was afraid to ask anybody for food."

Was Beatrice trying to put me on? I still wasn't quite sure about her.

"Then this very nice guy walks up to me and offers to help," Beatrice continued. "At first I thought he was a pimp. I didn't really know what a pimp looked like. On Sunset Strip you couldn't trust anybody. But

I found out I could trust Paco. He brought me here and helped me get set up. If it wasn't for him, I'd be dead, man."

"How come you have an apartment over by Sunset Strip, then?" I wanted to know.

"Oh. You see, Paco is a very kind person, and I didn't want to take up a bed here. He's always helping out people who are in trouble, just like he's trying to help you."

I began to feel a little better. I felt a little ashamed of myself, too. I guess I shouldn't have mistrusted Paco and Beatrice.

Beatrice put her arm around me. "I'll tell you what, I think Paco has an empty guest room right now. I know you're a little afraid to stay here, so I'll stay overnight with you. Would that make you feel better?"

That sounded good to me, so I agreed to stay. Something still didn't seem right, but I pushed the feeling to the back of my mind. These people had to be for real, I decided.

Beatrice took me up to the second floor and down the hallway. She opened the door to a beautiful room. I knew I could get to like this place.

That evening we had dinner together. There must have been ten girls around the big dining-room table. Some of them were very talkative and some were quiet. But I never did see that girl with the bruises. After dinner I asked Beatrice about her.

Beatrice put her finger up to her lips. "Shh. Don't get nosy."

I wished Beatrice hadn't said that. I had almost controlled my fear, and now this. Why would she say that?

"Hey come on, will you?" I protested. "Don't be so secretive. I thought this was a place where girls could come and stay."

"Of course it's a place for girls to stay," Beatrice agreed, "but some people here don't understand what's going on, and I forgot to tell you that. Just don't ask questions, okay?"

"It's not okay," I said. "I just wish you'd level with me, Beatrice. Something seems to be wrong about this place."

Beatrice put her arm around me and said, "Come on, let's walk out by the swimming pool. We can talk there."

We walked out to the patio and down a few yards to the swimming pool. It was beautiful.

We pulled up two lawn chairs and sat down. Maybe now Beatrice would tell me what was going on.

"Listen, Paco is a very private man," Beatrice began. "He makes lots of money, but he's very charitable and kind to many people. There are some people who don't understand what Paco is really doing, so he doesn't want people asking questions. All right?"

"But, Beatrice, I just have to confess I'm scared about this place. What makes me so nervous? Why should I be so afraid? Here I am in this beautiful mansion with a swimming pool. The food's great, everybody's kind to me, but still I'm nervous. Why am I so jumpy?"

Beatrice laughed. "You're uneasy because it's a strange place. That's all. You'll get used to it. That's exactly how I felt, at first, but not anymore. I usually come and spend weekends here. It's fabulous. Relax, Kari, just relax."

Beatrice got up. "I have to go to work, but I'll be back later on tonight. Why don't you go to bed early and get a good night's sleep?"

That sounded strange. I thought Beatrice was a secretary. "You work at night?" I asked.

Beatrice laughed again. "Yeah, I work at night."

"What kind of work do you do?" I persisted.

"Well, I'm in a service business which helps people out," she told me.

"What do you mean, helping people out? You don't work at some shelter feeding hungry people, do you?"

Beatrice laughed once more. It seemed as though everything was funny to her. I didn't know whether to laugh or keep probing. I decided to ask one more question.

"Beatrice, are you a prostitute?" I asked.

Before I saw it coming, I felt a sting on my cheek. Beatrice had slapped me. "Kari, I don't want you ever to say that word again! I am not a prostitute. I'd never subject my body to animal behavior like that. I am not. Do you understand what I'm saying?"

Now I felt embarrassed. But I wasn't going to give up. "Then why are you so vague about what you're doing?" I countered. "Why are you so mysterious about this place? I have a sneaking suspicion that Paco is a pimp and you're a prostitute. I also feel very strongly that those girls around the supper table were prostitutes, too. Now that's how I feel. If you want to hit me again, go ahead."

Beatrice glared at me. I glared back. She whirled around and stomped off without another word.

I stood there watching her go into the big house. A couple of minutes later Paco came out. He headed straight for me. I started backing up. Had Beatrice said anything to him? I wanted to run for my life. I really felt scared now.

Paco got closer. I turned and started to go the other way, but he grabbed my arm and spun me around. I expected to get slapped again. Or if Paco was a pimp, maybe I'd get killed. I held my breath.

Paco just stared at me for a while, then he said, "Beatrice was furious. She claimed you called her a prostitute. Is that right?"

What was I going to do now? If I said yes, would Paco try to kill me?

The best thing to do was apologize. "I'm sorry," I quavered. "I guess I did accuse Beatrice of being a prostitute. I know I shouldn't have said it."

"Why would you accuse her of something like that?" Paco demanded.

"I don't know. I just don't know. All of a sudden it came out. I'm scared, Paco, really scared. Here I am three thousand miles away from home, and I meet you and Beatrice and come to this place, and things

just don't add up, and I'm scared." I was blubbering
by now. Hot tears rolled down my cheeks.

Paco put his arm around me. "Kari, sometimes I
just can't understand people. I'm quite a prosperous
businessman, and I open my home to runaways. But
every once in a while I get someone who judges my
motives. I'm an honest, decent, hard-working man,
and here I get all these accusations. And to accuse a
girl like Beatrice. I'm really ashamed of you, Kari. I
understand your fears, but you don't need to lash out
at innocent people like that."

Paco's gentle rebuke made me feel terrible. "I'm
sorry, Paco," I told him. "I'll apologize to Beatrice."

"Do you know why she got so angry?" Paco asked.

"Yeah, I wouldn't want to be called a prostitute
either," I admitted.

"Well, it's more than that," he said. "I don't know
if Beatrice told you or not, but she ran away from San
Francisco and ended up on Sunset Strip. I got to
know her and found out that her mother is a prostitute in San Francisco. Beatrice vowed that she'd
never become a prostitute. So when anybody starts
mentioning anything about prostitutes, she goes into
a tizzy. I guess it's kind of a reflection on her mother,
and she is embarrassed by that. The very word makes
her mad."

Paco and I walked back toward the house. "Do you
care for a drink?" he asked.

"You don't mean something strong like whiskey,
do you?"

Paco smiled. "I have anything you want. I've got

orange juice, apple juice, water, whiskey, cocktails, beer, wine. Anything you want."

I was too young to start drinking alcohol. I had tried it a few times before but never had liked the taste.

We walked into the living room, and Paco walked across to a well-stocked bar. He poured two drinks. I couldn't read the label on the bottle because his back was to me.

Paco walked over and handed me a glass. I reached out to grab it. Then I knew what was going to happen. Something was in that drink to knock me out. My suspicions were probably true. He would knock me out and take advantage of me. "Oh, Paco, I don't drink," I said nonchalantly.

He laughed. "Listen, this won't give you a heart attack. Just drink it slowly. It'll make you feel good."

"Now, my mother told me never to drink," I said. "I guess that stayed with me."

My heart was beating like crazy by now. Somehow I had to get out of this place.

Would Paco grab me and force it down my throat? I waited to see what would happen next.

He slowly put the drink down on a table. I felt better. Then he said, "Do you want to smoke a joint, then?"

"Hey, what's going on here anyway?" I asked. "First the booze and now the pot. I really only snort cocaine." I don't know why I said it. I guess I was trying not to show how nervous I really was.

"Well, I'm certainly glad you do something," Paco

said approvingly. "Stay here. I'll be right back."

In a few minutes Paco reappeared with a little packet in his hand. It didn't take me long to figure that one out. I knew what it was. Cocaine. "Anything you want, Kari, we have it here," Paco said.

He sat down next to the big table and brought something out of a drawer. I watched him take the white stuff out of the cellophane bag and put it on a piece of glass. Then he took out a tiny spoon.

He put some cocaine up his nose and snorted. This was the first time I'd ever seen anything like it.

He looked up at me. "Want to try some?"

I'd heard a lot about cocaine. It was supposed to be the rich person's drug. Something inside possessed me, and I said, "Yeah, I'll try some."

I sat down next to Paco. He took the little spoon and dipped it into the white powder. Then he lifted it up to my nose. "Slowly, and I mean slowly, inhale with your nose."

I inhaled slowly. Then I felt it.

The next second it hit me. I cannot describe what happened. It felt as though I were actually floating above the ground. There was a moment of ecstasy and feeling that I can't describe with words.

Then I started to laugh. Paco reached out and hugged me. I hugged him back.

We snorted some more. Something in me said that this is what I wanted. It took away all my fear. It took away all my inhibition. Cocaine was the answer!

After we had snorted, we went down the hall to where Paco had an elaborate game room. He had a

pool table, Ping-Pong tables, computerized games—
you name it. I don't know how many hours I spent
there, but it was such a wonderful feeling. And it was
all free. No need to put quarters into the machines—
just push a little button.

When I finally got sleepy, I told Paco I was going to
bed. He just smiled. I was hoping he wouldn't follow
me. He didn't.

My room had its own private bathroom. I took a
shower and crawled into bed. Someone had even laid
out some clean pajamas for me. This seemed almost
like heaven.

The next thing I knew it was morning. The sun was
shining through the windows, and the birds were
singing. I felt great.

When I got downstairs, there was no one around. I
guess everybody was sleeping in. Maybe rich people
lived like that.

There were a couple of maids in the kitchen. I went
in and said, "Hey, where is everybody?"

One of the maids looked at me. "Oh, didn't they
tell you? Everybody keeps late hours here. Nobody
gets up until around noon. Then you can have either
breakfast or lunch. What would you like?"

"What time is it?" I asked.

"About ten o'clock," she said. "It's still a while before we normally eat, but I'd be glad to fix you up
something."

I was hungry, so I said, "How about eggs and
toast?"

"Coming right up. Would you like some orange juice, too?" I nodded. That sounded good.

While my breakfast was cooking, I explored a little. This mansion had three big living rooms. I wondered why rich people had so many.

In a few minutes the maid came and got me. She sat me down at the table. The dishes were very elaborate and the silverware was sterling. I felt rich, and wanted this feeling forever.

I ate my breakfast, and then went out to the patio next to the pool. Everything seemed so quiet and peaceful. I just couldn't imagine why I had been so afraid the night before.

At noon some of the girls got up. They really looked as though they'd had a rough night. I wondered what had happened to them.

Then I wondered about Beatrice. I knew I had to apologize to her.

Around 12:30 they served lunch. There was no Beatrice. "Hey, where's Beatrice?" I asked Paco. "Oh, she's not around today," he said. "She's back at her apartment."

"Oh, that's too bad. I was going to apologize to her."

Paco patted my hand. "I saw her last night and told her how sorry you felt. She seemed to take it okay. She told me to tell you to forget it, all right?"

That made me feel better. At least Beatrice wasn't mad at me anymore.

"Upstairs, in the hallway, you'll see a closet," Paco said. "I have some new swimming suits in there for the girls. Why don't you pick out one for yourself and go swimming. You can get a nice California tan."

That sounded good to me! I hurried upstairs and found the closet. Sure enough, there were some beautiful swimsuits. I picked one that I hoped would fit.

When I put it on, I was a little embarrassed. It was a two piece that looked more like one piece had been cut in half. It exposed quite a bit of me.

I thought I might as well get over my inhibitions, though. Besides, I was enjoying this place.

When I got back to the pool, Paco was sitting there in a lounge chair. He had his bathing suit on, too.

He looked at me and smiled. "Hey, Kari, you have a beautiful figure, babe. I mean, you're beautiful!"

That embarrassed me. I saw his eyes going up and down my body, and I felt kind of daring. I started to strut, swinging my hips.

Paco laughed. "Hey, kid, you're all right." I walked over and sat down next to him. He said, "With a body like that, you can make lots of money."

What did he mean by that? I still had it stuck in my mind about Paco's being a pimp. I just couldn't get it out.

Paco went on. "I'm sure you know that many movie stars are movie stars because of their bodies. Most models are successful because of their bodies, and I think you've got what it takes."

That was better. At least he was thinking of my being an actress or a model, and not practicing that other occupation I had accused Beatrice of doing.

Paco didn't stay around much longer. He got up

and said he had business to take care of. I stayed in the sun too long and got a wicked sunburn.

Most of the girls were there for dinner. It was a delicious meal. I tried to ask the girls what they did, but all of them said about the same thing. They were in a service business.

Finally I pulled one of the girls aside after we'd left the table. "Come on, now. Tell me exactly what you do," I demanded.

Her face turned white. She quickly looked one way and then the other. "Don't you know what's going on around here?" she asked.

"All I know is that I ran away and ended up on the Sunset Strip, and Paco and Beatrice picked me up and brought me here," I told her. "Why?"

"Don't you know why you're here?"

"I'm here because I'm a runaway, I guess. Beatrice started talking to me, then Paco came by, and here I am. That's exactly what happened."

"Well, I've got to be going," she said. "Can't talk to you now."

I took hold of her arm and said, "Hey, level with me, will you. What is this place?"

"Listen, you little brat," she hissed. "If you're not smart enough to know what's going on around here by now, you're the most stupid person alive. I mean, you are stupid!"

All my fears flooded through me. Was this really a bunch of prostitutes and a pimp?

"Just level with me," I begged. "Tell me what this

place is. If it is what I think it is, I'll get out of here and never tell anyone you told me, okay?"

The girl snatched her arm away. "Got to go now." She hurried off down the hall. I turned around, and then I gasped. There stood Paco.

"What are you talking about?" he asked. "What did you say to Sylvia?"

I didn't like the way Paco said that. I made an excuse. "I was just asking her how to get more cocaine. That cocaine last night was great."

Would Paco believe me? I waited. "Kari, I hope you're not trying to pry into my personal business," Paco said slowly. "Are you?"

"Oh, no, Paco. I'd never do that," I said quickly. "I can't thank you enough for rescuing me from the street. The cops probably would've gotten me and put me in jail, or worse yet, I'd have to go back home to my mother and violent stepfather. You know that stepfather of mine raped me? I mean, he's a monster."

My mind was racing wildly. I hoped my story was working. I waited for Paco to respond. He just glared at me.

"Listen, is there anything I can do to pay you back?" I said desperately. "I mean, you've been so good to me. What can I do for you?"

Paco started to smile. His smile turned into a wide grin. Then he said, "As a matter of fact, I just wanted to talk to you about that. Come on, let's go into my study."

Paco put his arm around me. We headed toward the study. I should never have gone there. What Paco was about to tell me would change my life—for the worse.

4

The study had so many books, it looked like a library. At one end was a very large desk. There were lots of antique chairs around and a couple of huge lounges. The whole room was overwhelming.

Paco pulled me toward a lounge. "Sit down, Kari. I want to have a little talk with you."

"Why? Did I do something wrong?" I asked.

Paco smiled. "Well, not really, but I think it's time you and I had a talk."

I was braced for the worst. Was Paco a pimp? I sat down on the lounge, and Paco sat in a chair next to me. He said, "I suppose you're really wondering what I do, aren't you?"

That was one question I didn't want to answer at all. I'd better play dumb. "Paco, I don't really care what you do," I told him. "All I care about is that you picked me up and took care of me. The last couple of days you've treated me like a princess. You fed me well. You gave me a beautiful room. And I want to thank you for it. That's all I care about."

"I've done it for a purpose," Paco said. "Do you know what that purpose is?"

My heart started beating faster. I knew what was coming. I gritted my teeth. "You're a pimp, and you want me to be your prostitute," I said. Then I waited for Paco to flatten me.

"Well, I don't look at it that way," Paco said calmly.

"Then how do you look at it?" I demanded.

"Well, Kari, let's just suppose that Beatrice and I hadn't come along. Where would you be?"

I thought about it. "Probably still out on the street."

"Nope. You would not be out in the street. You'd probably be in a dingy, filthy room tied to a chair."

"You mean somebody would have kidnapped me?"

"Worse than that. There's a bunch of mean, vicious pimps out there who are waiting for young girls like you. With your gorgeous face and thin body, you'll bring a very high price. But you have to pay for it."

What was he talking about? "You want to run through that again?" I was incredulous. "You mean someone would actually kidnap me and beat me up?"

Paco nodded and said, "That's exactly what I mean. Whether you realize it or not, I've actually saved your life."

I stared at Paco. What were pimps really like? I understood they were wild, vicious, and mean. So far, Paco wasn't playing that part. I said, "You're just trying to set me up for something, aren't you?"

"You're an innocent little girl, Kari. You don't know what life is really all about yet. But Sunset Boulevard is a vicious place, and I mean vicious. Young girls like you can easily lose their lives. Girls are bought and sold by pimps. Pimps kill each other for girls."

The more Paco talked, the more afraid I became. How did I ever get myself mixed up in this? I finally said, "Well, I want to thank you, Paco. I think I'll just be going now."

"That's an interesting statement," he said. "Where do you expect to go?"

I thought for a moment. I really didn't know. Then I said, "Down to the beach."

Paco laughed. "I guess you don't quite understand what I'm trying to say."

"Well, what are you trying to say?" I asked. "I don't understand."

"You have two choices. You can leave here and end up in the hands of a vicious pimp. They'll find you no matter where you go. You're a runaway, and the pimps know it. Or, if you stay and work with me, I'll treat you right."

That was it. I had known it all along. I was to become a prostitute. I jumped up. "There is absolutely no way you're going to get me to work for you. I've heard about prostitutes. They end up with diseases! Besides, they're filthy and dirty."

Paco stood up, too. "You've seen the girls. Do they look like that?"

Then I thought about the bruised girl. "What about

that girl yesterday?" I asked. "Black and blue. I'll bet you beat her up, didn't you?"

"Listen, a deal is a deal. I promised that girl I would take care of her, and I took good care of her. She was just a wild kid from Phoenix, and I picked her up. But there's an understanding we have. She works for me. And nobody else."

"What do you mean by that?" I asked.

"Marcia tried working for another pimp," Paco explained, "so I had to teach her a lesson. She's got to obey the rules."

"You mean you beat her up, just like that?"

Paco nodded. "The girls are like wayward children. Sometimes you have to discipline them. I had to discipline Marcia, that's all. She's lucky she's still alive."

I didn't want any part of this life. I started to walk out of the room. Paco grabbed my arm. "You can't go."

"What do you mean I can't go?" I said. "Just watch me."

Paco lifted me right off the ground. "Have it your way. You can go." I half expected him to carry me to some room and start beating me, but he abruptly put me down. Then he said, "Before you go, here is something I want to give you." Paco reached in his pocket and pulled out a little white envelope. He handed it to me. One quick look and I knew what it was. Cocaine.

"Why are you giving this to me?" I asked.

"Well, I saw that you kind of liked it, so I thought maybe you could have another bag of it. No charge this time."

I looked at Paco. Not only was he a pimp, but he might be a cocaine dealer as well. Maybe that's how he had gotten this huge estate.

Paco said, "Come over here, and let's snort together. I have plenty of it around."

Without giving me a chance to answer, he led me over to the desk. He pulled out a drawer and took out his spoon.

I didn't say another word. I snorted the whole bag. I had a quick flush, and all of a sudden I had no more problems.

At the height of my flush Paco said, "Kari, I need your help. You see, a good-looking girl like you could make herself a lot of money. I'll take real good care of you, and I promise you I'll never beat you. I'll take good care of you."

All of a sudden, prostitution didn't sound so bad. It sounded like a way of making lots of money.

Paco said, "How about working for me?"

In my high, I quickly said, "Why not?"

Paco threw his arms around me and kissed me very passionately. I didn't seem to care. In fact, it felt really good. Later that night I got into Paco's Rolls Royce and went to Sunset Boulevard with him.

We pulled up to a corner. There stood Beatrice. Paco yelled to her.

Beatrice walked over. As soon as she saw me, she smiled. That surprised me.

Beatrice said, "Kari, welcome to the world of living. I know you're going to do great."

I wasn't so sure. I felt as though I might need to snort another bag of cocaine.

I got out of the car, and Paco drove off. Beatrice said, "You'll probably have lots of customers with your good looks and body. Let me tell you what to do."

As we stood there on the corner, Beatrice gave me some quick lessons. "Try to get as much money as you can. Some guys will pay thirty dollars, and other guys will pay three hundred." There was no set charge for prostitution.

I guess I was still a little high from that cocaine. As she talked, I was surprised that I wasn't afraid.

When I felt the effects of the cocaine wearing off, I became more scared.

"Beatrice, I can't go through with this," I said. "I told Paco I would, but I want out. I've got to get away from here."

Beatrice said, "I know exactly how you feel. Come on with me. You'll feel better."

Beatrice led me down another block. We went up into an apartment. She had the key. Evidently this was hers.

We went inside, and then to the kitchen. Beatrice opened up a cupboard door and reached way back inside. I stood there and watched her. Then she pulled something out and laid it on the counter. She unraveled it. I knew what it was. I had seen pictures before. It was a set of works.

I stood there in amazement at what was happening. Beatrice had pulled a bag of dope out of her blouse.

She set it up, then she grabbed my arm. I jerked back. She said, "This'll get you up. After getting off, it'll help you. Cocaine's a quick flush, but this will stay with you for a while."

When I drew back some more, she said, "Listen, Kari, I'm telling you, take a shot of dope, and you'll feel better."

She grabbed my arm. I turned the other way. I felt the jab of the needle. And then I felt real light. The fear washed out. Beatrice was right! Getting high before taking on customers was the way to go. I started to rub my nose. The sensation thrilled me.

Beatrice loaded up and got off herself. She said, "Paco gives me my dope. I have to have it to work the street."

Beatrice put her works away. Then she put her arm around me. "You okay now?"

I was still feeling the effects of the high, and I was ready. The streets didn't bother me anymore. I was anxious to see how much money I could make for Paco. He was the one who would give me more dope.

When we got back out on the street, Beatrice explained to me more of what to do.

"Where do you take these guys?" I asked.

"You have three choices. Sometimes you take them to a hotel. Sometimes you can take them to my apartment. Or, you can use the car."

In a couple of minutes a car drove up. Beatrice said, "I'll take this one. Watch and you'll learn."

Beatrice walked up to the car. The guy said, "Hey, you ready to go out?" Beatrice jumped into the car, and they drove off. Beatrice was a professional. She didn't mess around.

A car drove up a few minutes later. There were two guys in it. They looked over at me. One of them said, "Hey, chick, how about it?"

Beatrice hadn't told me what to do about two guys. What now? I smiled uncertainly at them.

"Come on, babe, we'll pay you lots of money," the other guy said. I wondered what to do. I stood there smiling. The guys kept encouraging me.

Just then Beatrice walked up. She looked at the two guys, then she quickly grabbed my arm. "Let's get out of here!"

She pushed me down the street. I said, "Hey, what's the matter with you, anyway? Those guys were going to pay lots of money."

Beatrice didn't say anything. Then she pushed me into a coffee shop. We stood inside the door. Beatrice said, "Young lady, you were being propositioned by two detectives. Can't you tell a cop when you see one?"

"Are you kidding?" I yelled.

"Yeah, those are cops. Always be careful of two guys in a car. Cops usually travel in pairs. Watch for them. You hear me?"

I wasn't going to forget that one. All I needed was to get arrested—and for prostitution. Then I'd probably be sent back home. That would be worse than jail!

Beatrice kept staring out of the window of the coffee shop. I followed her gaze. The car was still there. "What are we going to do?" I asked her.

"Just stand here until they leave. Those cops won't come in here and bust us. They don't like to make a ruckus in a public place like this."

Beatrice was smart. I'd have to listen to her more carefully.

The car finally drove off. "Okay, it's clear," Beatrice said. "Let's go. But be careful."

We walked back out to the street and stood there. A guy walked up to us. He looked at Beatrice, and then he looked at me. He said, "Hi, there. What do you say?"

Beatrice nudged me. "I'm doing just fine," I mumbled. "How about you?" I shot a look at Beatrice. She was smiling. Evidently this wasn't a cop.

Beatrice said, "Hey, mister, want to have a good time?"

"Yeah, but not with you," he answered. "How about this young girl?" I looked at the guy. He looked kind of old—and kind of sloppy. I felt real squeamish.

Beatrice said, "You can have her for a hundred dollars."

The guy jumped back. "A hundred bucks! Are you kidding? No way, just no way."

Beatrice said, "Okay, fifty then, but no less. She's young, real young."

"All right, fifty it is," the guy agreed.

Beatrice handed me a key. I knew what that meant. We were to go to her apartment.

The guy was laughing and giggling as we went up to the apartment, but I was feeling horrible. And I was afraid again. I probably should have shot more than one bag of dope.

As soon as we got inside the door, I said, "Okay, mister, fifty dollars." The man reached into his pocket and pulled out his wallet. He counted out the money.

We headed toward the bedroom. It took a lot longer than I had hoped for. And it was terribly, terribly embarrassing. After it was over, I swore to myself I'd never do it again.

The guy got up and left the room. I was stunned.

As I sat there on the edge of the bed, I couldn't believe what had happened. Then I looked at my hand. I was still holding the fifty dollars. Then I thought, *it's not bad money if you can get over the shock.*

When I walked back out to the street, Beatrice started laughing. She said, "Well, what do you think?" I just stood there, staring at her.

"I don't want this anymore," I told her. "I'm getting out."

Beatrice said, "Kari, there's no getting out. You belong to Paco."

"Well, I'm going to walk down the street, and that'll be the end of it," I said. "I'm getting out of here. I got my fifty dollars, and I'm going! I'm getting out now."

I started to walk away. Beatrice grabbed me and jerked me back. "Look over there."

Beatrice was pointing across the street. I squinted. Leaning up against the building was a person. And then I saw who it was. Paco.

"Well, he'll never catch me," I said defiantly.

"Don't do anything stupid, Kari," Beatrice warned. "Paco's been through this many times. He knows what happens when a girl like you is on the street for the first time. She wants to run. He's there to make sure you don't run."

"What do you mean by that?" I demanded.

"If you take off, Paco is going to get you. He's armed with a forty-five automatic. He may kill you."

I just couldn't believe this. That didn't sound like the Paco I had talked to an hour or so before. "That's not what he said," I told Beatrice. "He said he'd take care of me."

"You'd better believe he'll take care of you. But on his own terms. You try to take off, and he's got another tactic he uses."

"What do you mean, another tactic? He won't lay a hand on me."

"Kari, let me tell you something. I used to be just like you. But I learned not to fight the system. It's better to go along with it and not get yourself hurt. Do you understand what I'm trying to tell you?"

"Well, he's not going to hurt me," I insisted.

"Okay, Kari. Look closely. I want to show you something."

Beatrice pulled out the neck of her sweater. "Look down in there," she said.

I leaned forward and looked. Across her chest was an ugly scar. It was about a foot long. I jumped back. "What happened?"

"I used to work for a pimp by the name of Hurricane. He's dead now. One time I tried to escape from him. He caught me and beat me, and then he took his big switchblade and started to cut me. He said if I ever tried escaping again, he'd kill me. I never forgot it."

My mouth dropped open. I couldn't believe this. Was Beatrice telling me the truth?

"I'm still not afraid of Paco," I said. I was really scared, but I didn't want to let Beatrice know.

"Kari, you'd better listen to me. I'm not saying Paco is going to take a switchblade and cut you, but I would never test him. You saw that girl who was beaten up, didn't you? She's lucky she's alive. Don't test Paco. Please don't."

I looked across the street to where Paco was standing, only he wasn't standing now. He had started walking toward us. I knew if I tried to run for it, he'd probably shoot me in the back. I decided to stand my ground.

Paco walked up. "Hey, something wrong over here?"

Beatrice said, "We're just having a little talk, that's all." I looked at Paco. He glared back at me and said to Beatrice, "How much did she make from that last guy?"

"I don't know," she replied. Then to me, "How much did you make?"

I had stuffed the money in my blouse, two twenty-dollar bills and a ten. But I wanted to keep some of it. I needed the money to get away. I said, "Only ten dollars."

As soon as I said that, Paco grabbed me. Then he jerked on my hair. "You gave yourself away for ten lousy dollars?" He shook me and screamed, "Where's the money?" I started to reach in my blouse, but he beat me to it. I felt him jerk the money out.

He smoothed it out. "There's fifty dollars here, not ten!" I started to say something, and then I felt the slap on my cheek. It stung. Paco slapped me again. "No filthy brat like you cheats on Paco. You understand that?"

He grabbed my blouse, twisted it, and picked me off the ground. When we were nose to nose, he spit. I felt the spit on my mouth.

Paco released his grip. I reached up and wiped off my mouth. He slapped me again.

I didn't know whether to cry or scream or what. I decided to just shut up. I didn't want to get him any angrier. Beatrice was right. He could kill me.

Paco stuffed the money into his pocket. "Don't ever cheat on Paco," he snarled. "Don't ever cheat. Do you understand that?"

Paco was pointing his finger right at me. I nodded my head. I knew I wouldn't cheat on him anymore— not on my life.

Paco said, "Give her another chance, Beatrice. But if she messes around, she's going to get it. Get it good."

Paco stomped across the street. I looked at Beatrice. She was as white as a sheet. She said, "Kari, you're lucky to be alive. Don't you ever cheat on your pimp. That's the law of the jungle. Cheat on your

pimp, and you're dead, I mean dead. Do you understand that?"

My eyes went across the street to Paco. He stood
with his hands on his hips, looking at me. I hated
him. But I was trapped. How could I ever escape?

5

What kind of life had I gotten myself into? I couldn't understand how Beatrice took it so casually. "Has Paco ever hurt you?" I asked her.

Beatrice gave a strange laugh. "Well, I guess there are various ways you could look at it. He's hurt me, and hurt me bad. But there's something inside of me that says I don't want to leave him. I mean, it's kind of strange, but I'd rather be out here on the streets than be a waitress at some cheap restaurant. I guess this is all I know."

"I don't understand that," I said. "It looks like you're working only for him. I mean, what do you do with your money?"

"The answer is obvious," she said. "I give it all to Paco."

I just couldn't believe it. This was slavery. "Well, that's not going to happen to me," I said resolutely.

Beatrice tugged on my blouse. "I have to warn you, Kari. Don't do anything rash. It's too dangerous. Play the game according to the rules, and you'll live. If you violate those rules, you're going to get killed."

"What rules are you talking about?" I asked.

"Just do what Paco says, and you'll live. Don't do what he says, and you'll get killed. It's that simple."

Somehow I had to get out of this. If I was ever to escape, I'd never, never, and I mean never, come back to this place! Maybe if I tried Florida or Texas, things would be better.

"I'll wait for my opportunity, and then I'm taking off," I told Beatrice.

She laughed. "That's what I used to think. But I got used to it. You'll get used to it, too, kid."

"I'll never get used to it! That experience with that old guy in your room was enough. I want out."

Beatrice laughed again. "You're trapped, Kari. Remember, don't break the rules."

I glared at Paco, standing across the street. He was the one who was making me do this. I had to think of a way out.

Then Beatrice said, "There was one girl who got out. Paco let her go."

That seemed strange. One moment Beatrice was saying I'd never get out, and now she was saying that I could. "What do you mean by that?" I asked.

"There was this girl by the name of Jill. She used to work for Paco. But Paco made a deal with her. She could buy her way out. It cost her thirty thousand dollars, though."

"Thirty thousand dollars?" I yelped. "I'll never get that much money!"

"You can if you work hard."

"What do you mean, work hard? I'll never, never get that much money."

"Well, I tell you what. A good-looking, young girl like you can make lots of money. Not only do you charge a fee for your services, but you can look for ways to steal money. When you get the chance to get money out of a guy's wallet, you take it. Any way you can get money, kid, you get it."

"But that's stealing," I said.

"Oh, get off of it, Kari. It's not stealing; it's just taking money. First of all, prostitution is illegal. The guy is committing an illegal act. Whatever happens beyond that isn't breaking the law. I mean, the whole system is breaking the law. But whatever you do within the system isn't breaking the law. Understand?"

I thought about it. I couldn't quite sort it out in my mind. Breaking the law was breaking the law, whether it be prostitution or stealing money.

"You'll catch on, Kari. You'll catch on. It takes a few days. But you'll get it."

"What do you mean by that?" I asked.

"After a while everything seems like a fog. I mean, you don't really sell your body cheap; you get the highest price. But after you get your money, there's something that kind of snaps inside of you. You want to get back at the guy. So out of that bitterness, you do anything you can to steal from him. In fact, I've seen some girls freak out and cut the guy."

This was getting worse. I was getting more and

more afraid. I couldn't believe I had gotten myself
into this mess!

Beatrice said, "I'll walk across the street and talk to
Paco. I'll see if you can buy yourself out. Okay?"

My hopes began to brighten. Maybe I could earn
the money and get out—get out for good.

Without waiting for an answer, Beatrice walked
across the street to Paco. I thought I'd better stay put.

They were talking back and forth, but I couldn't
hear them. Paco was throwing his arms around. He
got a little bit excited. But then I thought, could I
really trust Beatrice? She had lied to me at first. Why
wouldn't she lie to me again? Maybe she'd just said I
could get the thirty thousand and buy myself out.
Then, when I got the money, Paco wouldn't let me go.
Could I trust her?

A few moments later, Beatrice came back. She had
a big smile on her face. She said, "I've got good news
and bad news."

"Don't play games with me, Beatrice. You know
what I want. I want out."

"Well, here's the good news. You can get out."

"Great!" I jumped up and down. "How much is it
going to cost me?"

"That's the bad news. It's going to cost you fifty
thousand dollars."

"Fifty thousand! How in the world am I going to
get that?"

"I know you're new to this, Kari, but it won't take
you long. There's a lot of old men who want young
girls. In fact, you'll do a lot better than I will. Here I

am, thirty-five years old, and kind of worn out. But a lot of guys want teenagers."

I wondered how much I could make in a month. Beatrice answered for me. "Kari, in thirty days you could probably get your fifty grand."

I stared at her. It didn't seem possible. Fifty thousand dollars in thirty days? That's six hundred thousand a year! Could I really make that much? And if I did, would Paco let me out?

But I knew I didn't have a choice. I'd have to try it anyway.

Cars started coming by. And I was busy, just as Beatrice had said.

The following night I wasn't as busy. Beatrice said business went up and down. If there were conventions in town, you got a lot of business. Other times it would depend on the weather. And Saturday night was the best night, of course.

Every time I came back to my corner, Paco would be standing there. He would reach out his hand, and I would give him all my money.

Then every night we'd go to his mansion. He'd pick up the other girls on the way. I had no idea how much money he was making, but the take must have been enormous.

Paco always made sure I was high before I went out on the street. Being high made it easier for me.

It was about a week later when I got into a car with a guy. It was a big Cadillac, and the guy looked as though he was rolling in dough.

I was taking the tricks to a spot a few blocks away.

We went up an alley and parked beside a deserted old building. It was private there. This way it didn't make the guys so nervous, and I could get business over quickly.

This guy was big, fat, and ugly. I was getting a bad attitude towards these tricks, anyway, just as Beatrice had said I would.

Beatrice even had me carry a switchblade. She said if I met a perverted old guy, I might have to use it. And I began to feel a desire to use my switchblade. The bitterness was there now.

We pulled into the alley and stopped. I told him what I had learned to tell all my tricks, "Business before pleasure."

The fat, old man reached for his wallet. As he pulled it out, I looked at it. It was stuffed with money. "How much?" he asked.

"A hundred dollars," I told him.

Without a moment's hesitation, he pulled out a hundred-dollar bill. My eyes got big. I couldn't believe how much he had in there. Somehow I had to get to it.

The guy started unbuttoning himself. I said, "Just a minute."

He stared at me. "You'll have to take off your pants and hang them out the window," I said.

"You want me to do what?"

"Take off your pants and hang them out the window."

The guy started to laugh. I laughed too. "Why do you want me to do that?" he asked.

"Well, there are cops patrolling the area, and they search any cars that are parked here," I lied. "There have been some robberies around here lately."

"You mean the cops are coming?" he gasped and started buttoning up.

"Relax," I said. "That's what I wanted to tell you. You see, I have a deal that I give half to the cops. But cops being what they are, we had to work out a signal so they wouldn't stop me. So every time a cop drives by and sees a car with pants hanging out the window, he doesn't stop. It's a pretty good system."

"Are you kidding?" he asked.

"Listen, you've heard about cops being bought off," I said. "You read the papers. Every once in a while they bust a cop or two for taking payoffs. Well, our deal is foolproof."

"I'm getting kind of scared," he told me.

"You don't need to be afraid of anything," I assured him. "We're in the safest place we could be. Not only will the cops not stop us, but they'll protect us. I mean, this place is safe. You don't have a thing to worry about."

He started to calm down. All I could think about was that big, fat wallet. And I was going to get it.

I reached over and put my arms around him. I had to get his mind off those cops. I held my breath and kissed him. I felt him relax. I had him now.

"Okay," he said. "I guess it'll be all right." He took off his pants and rolled down the window. Then he started to hang the pants out. It was kind of awkward.

"Let me help you," I offered. I straightened the

pants out so the wallet was right in front of me. "Let's hop in the backseat," I suggested.

Much to my surprise, the guy jumped over the front seat. It looked funny, and I almost laughed. But I bit my tongue. I didn't want to blow it.

As soon as he hit the backseat, he tried to get comfortable. It was time for me to act while he was wallowing around. I grabbed the pants and bolted out the door and down the street. I had his pants, his wallet, and all his money!

When I got to the end of the alley, I turned and looked. He had started running after me. Then he must have realized what he looked like and stopped in his tracks. That's when I burst out laughing.

I turned the corner and ran about four blocks more, where I took the wallet and threw the pants in a garbage can.

A taxi was coming down the street. I hailed it and jumped in.

The driver had evidently seen me running. "You seem to be in a big hurry," he said. "What happened?"

"Oh, nothing," I told him, "nothing at all."

The guy laughed. "Hey, I know what you're up to. Was it a perverted old man? Or was it the cops trying to get you?"

I leaned forward in the seat. "What did you say?"

The driver swung over to the curb, and then turned around and looked at me. "I said, you're a prostitute." I didn't like the way he said that. I didn't even like the word.

"You probably ripped off some john back there, didn't you?" he went on.

How did he know so much? And why had he stopped? I felt a little afraid.

Then he dropped his bombshell. "Okay, either you give me half, or I'll turn you in to the cops."

I couldn't believe this. The whole world seemed to be a big rip-off. Paco was ripping me off for fifty thousand, and now the taxi driver. I wasn't going for this one.

"Mister, you can be arrested for extortion," I said. "You can't get me like that."

"That's what you think, young lady. I'm throwing you to the cops."

The man reached back to grab me. I jammed my hand into my blouse and pulled out the switchblade. I snapped it open. At the click, I felt a surge of power in my hand. I looked at the guy. "Mister, you lay one hand on me, and I'll cut you up in little pieces. Nobody rips me off like that."

"I ought to kill you right now," he yelled.

Did I have the guts to stab this guy? I decided to try his arm. I brought my hand down as hard as I could. I felt the blade go into his arm. He jerked back and screamed.

Before he could make another move, I was out the door and running down the street, switchblade in hand.

Better put away my knife before somebody noticed it, I decided. I didn't want to throw it away. I knew I'd probably need it again.

I hurriedly folded the blade back into the handle. I put it into my blouse.

My mind was racing. Suppose that old man had me arrested for robbery. Or what if the taxicab driver had me arrested. It would be attempted murder.

But I kept thinking it couldn't happen that way. Certainly that old man wouldn't go to the cops. He was violating the law. He could be arrested for corrupting a minor. And the taxicab driver, he could be arrested for trying to rip me off. No, they couldn't go to the cops.

Just then I heard a siren coming my way. It was a patrol car with the lights blazing. I stopped. They had me! I quickly looked around. What could I do? Next to me was a grocery store. I hurried in. The police car stopped in front. The two cops were running my way. How did they know it was me?

I ran down a store aisle, then stopped and looked back at the cops. I didn't know which way to run.

The cops ran up to a counter. Then I noticed the crowd. Everybody was real excited. I stood there and watched. If the cops headed my way, I'd try to run for it. But where could I run to?

More people gathered around the cops. I was waiting for them to come after me, but they never did. Finally it dawned on me. Somebody must have tried to rob the grocery store. I looked down at my hand. I was still holding the guy's wallet. It looked loaded. No wonder that cab driver was going to get me. He had seen the big, fat wallet.

I took the wallet and pushed it in my blouse right

next to the switchblade. I looked down at myself. I really stuck out. I started to giggle. It was a nervous laugh, but I did look funny.

Then I slowly walked to the front of the store. The two cops had started out the front door. They had no one with them. Either it was a false alarm, or the guy had escaped. I was breathing easier now.

After the cops got outside, I very slowly walked out the front door. I didn't want to make any quick movements that would draw their attention. I got to the sidewalk and went to the right. Then I quickened my pace.

Halfway down the block I turned around. The police car drove off. I heaved a sigh of relief.

Now I only had to look out for that fat, old trick or the taxi driver. Maybe the taxi driver had learned his lesson. I hoped so. If he tried anything again, I'd do the same thing. Maybe I ought to get a gun, I thought.

It was still too far to walk back to Sunset. I had to get another taxi.

A taxi came along. I stared at the driver. He looked at me. Then he started to slow down. Did he know that I'd stabbed another taxi driver? I turned and quickly walked away.

Some of those taxi drivers had radios. Maybe the first one had radioed to be on the lookout for me. I had to think of a way out.

Then I noticed a clothing store that was still open. That was it. I would change clothes!

I hurried into the store and found a skirt and blouse, and then a new pair of shoes.

In the changing room, I pulled out the wallet. When I opened it up, I couldn't believe it. It was loaded with hundred-dollar bills. I felt an urge to count them right there, but if somebody came in, they probably would report it to the police. No young girl would have that much money on her.

As I pulled out a hundred-dollar bill, I had a crazy thought. Why didn't I just take the money, and get out of L.A.? But if Paco caught me, he'd kill me. I'd better wait. It wouldn't take long to pay him off at this rate. If he would let me go for fifty thousand, that is.

I went up to the counter to pay for the clothes. I told the woman I wanted to wear them out of the shop. When I gave her the hundred-dollar bill, her eyes widened. "Don't worry. It's not counterfeit," I told her.

The woman got embarrassed. "It seems strange—a young girl like you having a hundred-dollar bill," she said.

"My father is rich, okay?" I said sharply. I didn't want to play any games with this woman. "I'll have to get this okayed for change," was her reply.

That made me mad. I stamped my foot. "Are you trying to tell me my money's no good here? I ought to walk out of this store the way I am, clothes and all!" I tried to sound as mad as I could, but inside I was trembling. Suppose that money was counterfeit after all. If they searched me and found that other money, and that old man's wallet on me, I would go to jail for sure.

The woman started to walk away. She headed toward the back of the store. I couldn't take any more chances.

As soon as she got out of sight, I bolted for the front door. If the money was counterfeit, I was in trouble, anyway. If it was for real, she'd keep the change.

I hit the sidewalk running. At least now the trick and the cabbie wouldn't recognize me very easily.

It must have been about a mile back to the Strip, and I walked the whole way. I wasn't going to take any more chances with taxis.

When I finally got to Sunset, Paco was waiting. "Where have you been?" he screamed at me.

Before I could answer, he'd slapped me. "And what are you doing with different clothes on. You didn't go shopping, did you?"

"No, I didn't go shopping," I said tiredly.

"Then what are you doing with these clothes on? That's not what you left with a while ago. Are you cheating on me?"

Paco was making me mad. Here I'd almost gotten robbed, and I could have gotten killed by that taxi driver. But I didn't want to provoke Paco. I said, "Here, take a look at this." I reached in my blouse and pulled out the fat wallet. I handed it to Paco, and he opened it up. He sucked in a quick breath. "Where'd you get this?" he demanded.

"I don't know how much money is in there, Paco, but don't forget it goes against my debt."

Paco began to laugh. "Oh, yeah, I almost forgot."

"What do you mean, you almost forgot," I yelled. "A deal is a deal."

Paco turned and walked away. "It's a deal, isn't it?" I called after him.

Paco stopped and turned around to face me. He laughed. And he laughed some more. Then he turned and walked away.

My heart was beating like mad. Would Paco really let me out if I paid him fifty thousand dollars?

I had this crazy fear. I felt I was going to be his slave for life.

6

I'd been working for Paco for about a month now. I knew I must be getting close to my goal of fifty thousand dollars. Business was that good for me.

With all that money running through my hands, I was tempted to flee. But I knew Paco would find me. Every so often he'd tell me stories of girls who had tried to escape. He killed them.

Paco looked okay on the outside. It would be hard for me to believe that he would really kill somebody. I asked Beatrice about it a couple of times. Every time I mentioned killing, I saw fear in Beatrice's eyes. I knew Paco was capable of it then.

On a very busy Saturday night, I got through at about three o'clock in the morning. As Paco was taking us girls back to his place, I asked him, "A couple of more weeks and I should be at fifty thousand, shouldn't I?"

He laughed. It seemed as though every time I asked him how I was doing, he laughed. It was a very sinister laugh. "Yeah, Kari, you're getting closer."

"How close?" I asked.

"Hey, I only have to answer you once. I said closer, and that's it. Closer."

Paco's voice was rising. He was mad. I decided not to ask any more questions.

Another Saturday night, Paco dropped us off on the Sunset Strip. I got my first john, and when I came back, I waited for Paco. He was nowhere around. Beatrice was standing there. "Where's Paco?" I asked her.

She shrugged her shoulders. That was strange.

Then I picked up another guy. Again, I came back expecting Paco to be there, but he wasn't. Beatrice was nowhere around. Could this be my chance to run?

I went to the next block, where some of the other girls from Paco's stable were working. I asked them. None of them seemed to know anything, so I went back to my corner.

A car pulled up. I immediately knew who owned this one. It was Cowboy. I had heard about him. He was vicious. And it seemed as though all the girls who worked for him were mean. He seemed to delight in training the meanest ones.

He got out of his car and walked over to me. He smiled. I didn't smile back. He said, "Hey, babe, what you doing?"

We both knew I was working for Paco. There was a violent relationship between pimps on Sunset Strip. They hated each other. They tried their best to steal each other's girls. Sometimes it ended in death, only this time not the girl. One pimp would kill the other one.

"Cowboy, I would advise you to get in your car and drive off," I said. "Don't talk to me, you understand?"

He smiled again. His big white teeth glittered in the neon lights. "Hey, baby, don't treat me that way. I'll take good care of you, you hear?"

I turned my back on him. That didn't do any good. He took me by the shoulders and spun me around. "That guy Paco you're working for—don't you know he plans to kill you?"

"Kill me? No, he's not going to kill me. He treats me fine. I eat well. I sleep well. I live in a mansion, and I have a swimming pool. What else could a girl ask for?"

Of course I had all those things, but I had to pay a price for them—a horrible price.

"You should see the mansion I live in," Cowboy bragged.

"Of course you live in a big mansion, Cowboy. But you put your girls in a shack in East Los Angeles, down where the bums live."

"You're a smart little thing, aren't you?" I expected him to slap me. I looked up and down the street for Paco.

"You'd better get out of here. Paco's due back any minute, and if he sees you talking to me, you know what's going to happen to you."

"Paco's not coming back."

"What do you mean, he's not coming back?"

"The cops got him. It was the funniest thing you ever saw—Paco screaming and yelling, handcuffed to a police car. It was better than an old Abbott and Costello movie."

I stared at Cowboy. Was he telling the truth? It was true that Paco wasn't around. Was that what had happened?

Beatrice was standing across the street from me. I yelled over to her. "Cowboy says Paco got busted by the cops. Did you see what happened?"

She came running over. "Cowboy, are you lying?"

"No, I'm not lying. I saw it with my own two eyes. They hauled him away, all right."

"Beatrice, did you see anything at all?" I persisted.

She shook her head. "No. I've been out with a few guys, and it could've happened when I was out."

"Cowboy, you're lying," I accused. "I'm warning you. Not only are you talking to me, but you're talking to Beatrice, too. Paco is due back, and he's going to get you."

If I got rid of Cowboy, and it was true that Paco was busted, maybe this was my chance. I wouldn't have to wait to pay the whole amount of money. I would be free.

Just then a car drove up. Beatrice went over to it. Then she got in, and they drove off. It seemed as if Beatrice wasn't too worried about Paco. Maybe Paco was spying on me from across the street. I looked across the street. I couldn't see anyone. Maybe this was a trick. I knew I couldn't trust Cowboy.

Rachel, one of Paco's girls, was walking toward us.

When she saw Cowboy, she jumped back and said, "Cowboy, get out of here, man, or you're in trouble!"

"Rachel, do you know anything about Paco?" I asked.

"Yes, I know. The cops just busted him and took him away. But don't you move in on Paco's stable, Cowboy! I'm warning you. Get away from us."

Rachel walked down the street. Maybe I'd better get out of here, too.

I started to walk off. Then I felt it—right under my chin. It was a knife. Cowboy whispered, "Okay, girl, you're mine. Don't try anything funny, or I'll slice you up but good."

My heart was in my throat, and my knees felt weak. I was being kidnapped—by a pimp.

"I'm going to put the knife down, and we'll walk over to my car," Cowboy continued. "Be a good girl, and you'll live forever. Mess with me, and it's all over. Do you hear me, little girl?"

Cowboy lowered his knife, and I nodded that I understood.

Cowboy pushed me over to his car. He reached down and opened the door. "I'm getting in first, but I'm going to have hold of your hair," he told me. "If you try to run, I'll jerk you into the car and put my switchblade right in your heart."

I did just as he said. Cowboy slid across to the driver's side, and I got in with him. He reached across me and slammed the door shut. Then he started to laugh. I was too afraid to talk.

That's when I noticed someone standing right be-

hind Cowboy. Then I saw a gun. Cowboy's window
was open, and the person was pointing the gun right
at his head. "Well, if it isn't Cowboy," said a voice.
"And I caught him stealing."

I recognized the voice. It was Paco.

Paco leaned down and looked across at me. "Kari,
what are you doing in this car?" he demanded.

"You'd better ask Cowboy. He took a switchblade
to me and forced me in."

"Paco, that's not the way it is," Cowboy protested.
"I was driving by, and this girl here signals me. She
was giving me some sad story about your trying to
hurt her. She claimed you were going to kill her. I
told her there was no way could she work for me. I
got in the car and started to drive off, but she jumped
in. And then you showed up."

"Paco, he's a dirty, filthy liar," I screamed. I started
to open the door.

"Hold it right there, Kari," Paco ordered.

"Okay, I'm going to open this door, Cowboy, and
I'm going to slip behind you," he went on. "If you try
anything, I'm squeezing the trigger, and I'll splatter
your brains all over the windshield. Understand?"

Cowboy's eyes were big and round, and they
darted back and forth. He was scared to death.

Paco got in the backseat, the gun still pointed right
at Cowboy's head.

"Listen, Rachel came by, and Beatrice came by,
too," I told him. "Ask them, Paco. Ask them."

"She's lying," Cowboy interrupted. "You know

these girls; they'll lie their way out of anything. They can't be trusted."

"Ask Beatrice," I pleaded. "Beatrice wouldn't lie to you. Neither would Rachel. I'm telling the truth. I am!"

Paco glared at me. "You'd better be telling the truth, Kari. If you aren't, I'm going to plug both of you."

He settled back in his seat. "We'll just sit here a few minutes. When one of my girls comes by, we'll find out."

"Paco, someone said that the cops busted you," I said. "Is that where you've been?"

"Yeah, they busted me. I mean, they tried to bust me. They caught me with money. But it's just harassment. They're trying to make it tough on me. They tried to stick me with loitering, but I talked my way out of it."

I almost felt relieved. If had to make the choice, I would take Paco rather than Cowboy. I knew that Cowboy was out to tame me. I didn't like his name, and I didn't like his attitude. He was a real snake.

A car pulled up, and Beatrice jumped out. "Beatrice, come here!" I yelled.

Beatrice took a look at Cowboy's car. First she started to go the other way. Then I stuck my head out the window. "Paco wants to see you."

With that word she stopped. Paco leaned his head out the back window, "Come here, Beatrice."

What would I do if Beatrice didn't tell the truth?

Maybe she would tell a bunch of lies just to get rid of
me. I wasn't getting along with her that well lately. I
held my breath as she approached. She walked over
to Paco's side.

He said, "Cowboy here, tells me that Kari tried to
get out of pocket with me. He claims Kari wanted to
work for him. But Kari says she was forced to get into
his car at knife point. Did you see anything?"

"Beatrice, tell the truth." I was craning my neck to
see her face.

"I didn't see anything," Beatrice said.

"Beatrice, don't say that!" I screamed. "You know
as well as I do that a little while ago we were standing
on this street, and Cowboy came up to us. Now that's
the truth."

Beatrice shrugged her shoulders. I couldn't believe
it. Just then Rachel got out of a car. "Paco, there's
Rachel," I said. "She knows all about it."

Paco yelled to her, and Rachel came walking over.
I wasn't going to give Paco a chance to ask.

"Rachel, weren't you and I standing on the street,
and you were yelling at Cowboy?" I asked. "He tried
to get us away. Isn't that the truth?"

Rachel looked at Cowboy. She said, "You'd better
believe it. Cowboy tried to do us in, Paco. He tried to
do us in."

Paco said, "Rachel, are you telling the truth?"

"Paco, you got two liars on your hands," Cowboy
accused. "First Kari and now Rachel. The only one
you can believe is Beatrice."

Beatrice started laughing. She said, "Cowboy, I ought to take you out and kill you myself." Beatrice looked over at Paco. "Kari's telling the truth. Cowboy tried to make it with her."

"Cowboy, it's all over for you," Paco declared.

"Listen, Paco, times are tough for me," Cowboy whined. "I lost three girls. They got busted. I didn't know which way to turn."

Paco said, "Okay, Beatrice and Rachel, get back to work. I'll see you in a few minutes."

"What are you going to do, man?" Cowboy was frantic. "What are you going to do?"

Paco said, "Just start up the car and do what I say."

I opened the door to get out. Paco said, "No, Kari, I want you to stay. I think there's something you should learn."

What was Paco getting at? I was soon to find out.

We drove down Sunset Boulevard. Cowboy kept saying, "Easy, man. Go easy on me, Paco. Listen, tell me how much you want, and I'll pay you. I'll pay you now, man. I'll pay you now."

"How much have you got on you?" Paco asked.

As Cowboy was driving, he reached in his front pocket, and he pulled out a wad of bills. He handed them back. "That's everything I have. You can keep it all."

Paco stuffed the money in his pocket. He didn't even count it. "That's not enough," he said.

"Listen, I must have given you three thousand! How much more do you want?"

"I want fifty thousand," Paco told him calmly.

"Fifty thousand dollars! I don't have anything like that!" Cowboy wailed.

It seemed that Paco was always using the figure fifty thousand dollars. First, fifty thousand for my freedom, and now, fifty thousand for Cowboy's life. I wondered if Paco was ever going to let me go, for any price.

I didn't dare say anything, not at a moment like this. I wondered what Paco was going to do with Cowboy.

"Let's drive to downtown Los Angeles," Paco suggested.

That was strange. Why downtown? We drove on the freeway for a few miles.

When we got downtown, Cowboy said, "Okay, I'll tell you what. Just let me out, and you can have my car. This car is worth twenty thousand, easy."

"Nope," Paco replied, "I said fifty thousand, and that's what it is. Fifty Gs."

"Okay, okay, it's a deal," Cowboy said. "I'll get it for you tomorrow."

"Not soon enough. I want it now."

"Paco, don't talk like that," Cowboy protested. "I just gave you all the cash I had on me! Here, take this."

Cowboy slipped a big diamond ring off of his finger. He handed it over his shoulder. Paco took it and stuffed it in his pocket without looking at it.

"That ring is worth ten thousand," Cowboy said. "Those are huge diamonds on it. Huge diamonds."

"Not enough. I said fifty grand, and right now!"

Cowboy slipped off his watch. I looked at it. It was gold. He said, "Okay, man, my watch. This is a five-thousand-dollar watch. Take it."

Cowboy handed it over his shoulder. Paco grabbed it and stuffed it in his pocket. He didn't even pay attention to it. I knew something drastic was going to happen to Cowboy. No amount of money was going to stop Paco from whatever he was going to do.

Paco said, "Okay, let's drive to South Los Angeles."

"No, no! Don't do this! Don't do this!" Cowboy was pleading.

I wondered why I was along. If Paco was going to do Cowboy in, why bring me? Then I got scared. Maybe Paco was going to do me in, too.

We drove quite a few more blocks. We were getting near some old warehouses when Paco said, "Okay, turn left at this street."

Cowboy started screaming. Then he started crying. "Please, Paco! Please. Man, I told you I'd pay you! I'll get you the cash, I promise."

"Keep driving. And don't say another word. You understand that?"

Cowboy nodded. I looked at him. Big tears were streaming down his face. Was I about to witness a murder?

We drove a couple more blocks. Paco said, "Okay, turn to the right."

It was late at night and desolate. There wasn't a soul around.

Now we were near some dilapidated buildings. There was nobody in sight.

Paco said, "Okay, stop here."

"What are you going to do, Paco?" Cowboy quavered.

"I told you to shut up!" Paco snapped.

The car stopped. "Okay, woman. Get out of the car," Paco commanded. "Cowboy, you do what I say, or I'll empty this gun in your head."

For sure I was going to do exactly what Paco said. I wondered about Cowboy.

Paco leaned over the front seat and opened the door. He slid out with the gun still at Cowboy's head.

"What shall I do?" I asked.

Paco said, "You come with us."

I opened the door. At least I didn't have a gun at my head. But I kept wondering what was going to happen. If Paco killed Cowboy, would he kill me, too?

Paco pointed at a building. "Okay, both of you over there."

My pulse was thudding in my ears. "Kari, march in front of me," Paco ordered. My knees began to feel weak.

We marched up to the building—Cowboy first, then me, then Paco with the gun. The doors were torn off. "Okay, march inside," Paco said.

Cowboy was starting to slow down. I stepped in front of him. We walked into the building.

It was dark. The only light was streaming through broken windows down the side.

"Okay, Cowboy, on your knees!" Paco snarled.

I turned around and stared at Paco. Cowboy began to plead and cry. "No! No! No, Paco, please! Please! I'm worth more to you alive than dead. I'll get you the fifty thousand!"

Paco said, "Shut your mouth, Cowboy! No more yelling."

Then he turned to me. "Okay, Kari. I want you to stand behind me and look the other way."

I quickly stepped around Cowboy. I got behind Paco and stared toward the doorway.

And then it happened. There was one shot. I expected to hear a scream, but all I heard was a body hitting the floor—Cowboy's body.

Then I heard another gunshot, and then three more. I stood frozen in my tracks. Paco grabbed my arm. "Quick, let's get out of here."

We both ran out of the building and over to the car. We jumped in, and Paco turned the key. We spun out of there, tires squealing. The area was so desolate, I'm sure nobody had heard the shots.

Paco worked his way back to the freeway. As we got on the ramp, Paco looked at me.

"Kari, I'm not going to apologize for what I did to Cowboy," he told me. "He had it coming to him. But I just want you to know this. If you ever try to double-cross me, what I did to Cowboy, I'm going to do to you. You understand?"

My mouth fell open, and I felt as though I couldn't catch my breath. I knew Paco would do that to me. I wondered if I would ever try to escape.

When we got back to the Sunset Strip, Paco pulled up to the curb.

He reached over and opened the door for me and said, "Okay, get out there. And make it big. You're behind on your money to me."

As I turned to step out, I felt Paco's hand on my shoulder. He pushed hard. I went sprawling out the door and hit the pavement. I heard Paco laugh behind me.

I landed on my elbows and chin. It hurt. I started to look up. Standing before me was Beatrice. I looked at her. I hated her. She had almost gotten me killed. She was a filthy liar.

Paco drove off. I glared at Beatrice. "You're lucky to be alive," she told me.

I wondered about that. Could death be any worse than the way I was living?

7

Beatrice was always on my back. She was either yelling that I was taking her customers or that I wasn't working hard enough.

One evening I had finally had it. I went up to her and said, "Beatrice, you take care of your business, and I'll take care of mine."

She tried to slap me, but I avoided her. I felt a surge of anger, and I reached into my blouse. I was going to cut her with my switchblade.

Beatrice knew what was coming. She grabbed my arm and twisted it behind my back. "One girl tried that once, and I killed her," she snarled. I looked at her over my shoulder. "I'll tell you something," she went on. "I'd kill you, too."

"All right, you proved your point," I said. "Now let go of my arm."

She released my arm and pushed me. I stumbled and fell to the pavement. The anger came back, and I jumped up.

"Don't try anything foolish," Beatrice warned.

She must have been reading my mind, for my hand

had instinctively gone for my switchblade. I was surprised at myself. I was becoming a mean hooker.

Beatrice started to walk off. "Mess with me, and
I'm telling Paco," she flung at me.

"You can tell Paco, and you can tell the mayor and
the police chief," I yelled back. "Just get off my case,
girl!"

Beatrice spun around and glared at me. "You sure
have a fast mouth, sister. Maybe I should loosen a
few teeth for you, huh?"

Just then Paco drove up. I started toward his car,
and so did Beatrice.

Both of us started yelling at once. Paco got out and
held up his hand. "Okay, you two. I don't want
yelling, I don't want threats, and I don't want you
cursing each other out. I just want you to go to work.
Understand?"

I looked at Beatrice, then back at Paco. Paco
stepped up to me and put his arm around me. "Kari,
stay healthy. You're very valuable to me."

Sure, I knew how valuable. It was my body and his
money. The more money I made, the happier he
seemed to get.

Paco got back in his car, and Beatrice and I
watched him drive off. "Paco's in love with you,
Kari," Beatrice said suddenly.

I laughed. "I may be dumb, but I'm not stupid. He
loves my body, that's all. He knows it's a valuable
piece of merchandise. My body makes him lots of
money."

"You've got Paco all wrong," Beatrice insisted.

"He told me last night that he caught himself falling in love with you."

Well, the feeling certainly wasn't mutual! Every so often I thought about getting married, settling down, and having children, but Paco would be the last candidate on my list. If I had to marry him, I'd shoot myself in the head at the wedding.

"Well, if you and he talk tonight, just tell him I'm not available," I said to Beatrice. "I'm not in love with him. I'm not in love with anybody."

A strange thing was happening to me. I almost accepted the idea that I was a prostitute, and I rarely thought about buying myself from Paco. This change scared me.

I knew this kind of life couldn't last forever. Someday I would probably get arrested or killed, but I didn't seem to be as afraid as before.

One night when Paco took us girls to the street, he didn't stop at my usual corner. I knew something was wrong.

Finally, the next to the last girl was let out. Then it was only Paco and me. I had better find out what was up. "Something wrong?" I asked.

"Well, yes and no. I've got some problems with Beatrice."

"What kind of problems?"

"You remember that pimp by the name of Ripper?" I nodded. "Well, I saw him and Beatrice talking the other night."

Now I was in a jam. Should I try to defend Beatrice? Beatrice hated me, and this might be my chance to get back at her. I decided not to, though.

"I'm sure Beatrice is loyal to you, Paco," I said. "She's never said a bad thing about you."

"Beatrice is trying to set me up, Kari," Paco replied, shaking his head. "I have a sneaking suspicion she wants to get me and Ripper into a fight. I think she wants me killed."

Beatrice was a double-crosser. I knew that. She'd almost gotten me killed once. But why Paco? "Do you really think she'd try to do that?" I asked.

"Something's happened to Beatrice," Paco told me. "I don't know if she's getting too old, or what. She has a short temper. She comes to me and tells me all kinds of stories about the girls. Even about you, Kari."

Beatrice did have a big mouth. But why was Paco telling me all this?

Paco put his arm around me. Here it came. I hoped he wasn't proposing marriage!

"Can you do me a favor, Kari?" he asked.

I had a sudden thought. I said, "Whatever I do for you, can I buy myself out and leave you?"

Paco looked at me. "What do you mean, buy yourself out?"

"The fifty thousand dollars you placed on my head, that's what I'm talking about."

Paco laughed. "You're worth more than fifty thousand! Who would place fifty thousand on your head?"

Something was wrong. "That's what Beatrice told me," I said. "She said I could buy out for fifty thousand dollars."

Paco laughed. "I do remember Beatrice mention-ing something about that. But we both laughed about it. Beatrice knew I wasn't serious. Buying your way out from a pimp just doesn't happen, baby. Nobody buys their way out from a pimp."

I couldn't believe it. The whole thing had been a trick to get me to work hard. How would I ever get away from Paco?

Paco got real serious then. "I want you to go and talk to Ripper. I'll catch you two, and then I'm going to do Ripper in. That'll solve the whole problem."

"What if I don't go along with your plan?" I asked.

Paco dug his fingers into my shoulder. "I wouldn't push me too far, Kari."

His eyes were full of anger. I'd better go along with his plan and try to figure a way out later.

"Suppose Ripper knows it's a scheme to get back at him," I said. "What then?"

"Don't worry about that. I'll be watching the whole time. You'll never be out of my sight."

I didn't like this idea. I knew I would be flirting with death. Something could go wrong. "Why don't you ask one of the other girls to help you out?" I sug-gested. "You know, a girl like Elisa. Maybe she'd help you."

Paco tightened his grip on my shoulder. "I said I wanted you. Now, no arguments."

First Paco requested, then he demanded. I knew I had to do whatever he wanted. I said, "Whatever you do, Paco, don't let me out of your sight. I've heard all about Ripper and his hook. That hook is sharper than a switchblade."

"I know. I know. I've seen a few girls after Ripper got through with them. It wasn't a pretty sight."

Why did Paco have to tell me that? I started to tremble. Suppose Ripper was waiting for me and knew this was a scheme to get him murdered. "I'm really scared to death, Paco," I said. "Something could go wrong."

"Well, since you mentioned Elisa, I'll have both of you go together."

That made me feel better. I knew two would be better than one. "How are you going to set this up?" I asked.

"I have an apartment just off Sunset. I'll take you girls there, and I'll plant the word that you're there. Ripper will probably come and break into the apartment. Just stay cool, and everything will be okay."

"But you told me you'd be watching me all the time," I protested. "You said I wouldn't be out of your sight."

"Well, since the two of you are going to be together, I won't need to keep you in sight. But I'll be close by. Don't worry about a thing."

No matter what he said, I knew I was in trouble. "Paco, isn't there some other way you can do this?" I pleaded.

"You don't have a choice in the matter, Kari," he snapped. "Now shut up and do what I say!"

I didn't want to provoke Paco any more. I'd better

keep my mouth shut. We turned around and headed back down Sunset Boulevard.

Elisa was working a couple of blocks away. We pulled up, and Paco motioned her inside. She jumped in the backseat.

"I decided to give you both a night off, so I'm letting you use one of my apartments."

"Hey, that's great," Elisa said excitedly. "I was a little tired, anyway."

If she only knew. I bet if I were to mention the name *Ripper,* Elisa would jump out of the car and run for her life.

We got to Paco's apartment. It was very luxurious. But no matter how nice it looked, I was scared.

Paco went to the door. "Okay, Kari, just stay cool and do your thing."

Elisa looked at me. I looked back at Paco and said, "Sure, we'll enjoy the evening off together."

Paco shut the door and went out. Elisa came over to me and grabbed me by the shoulders. She shook me. "Hey, you're not going to do me in, are you?"

"No, Elisa. Just relax. Everything will be fine."

Elisa knew something was up. Should I tell her? If I did, and she took off, Paco would probably kill me. I decided to make up a story.

"Paco found out that the cops were going to bust you and me tonight," I lied. "He's got some guy in the police department that he's paying off for information. That's why we're here."

Elisa sighed. "Wow, sure glad you told me that. I

just got through doing six months. Baby, I don't want
to go back in there again."

"What were you in for?" I asked.

"Aw, they got me for drugs. I did a stupid thing. I
had a packet of dope on me."

Paco was supplying most of his girls with dope. Not
only did he sell us, he also dealt in drugs. I'm sure he
didn't miss the dope he gave us.

Elisa changed the subject. "Why don't we watch
TV for a while?"

"Yeah, that's a good idea," I agreed.

Elisa went to the refrigerator next. "Do you think
Paco would mind if we had something to eat?"

I wasn't hungry. I could feel the pain in the pit of
my stomach. Any moment now Ripper would be
coming. But I might as well not spoil it for Elisa.

"I'm sure Paco doesn't mind," I told her. "With his
money, he could buy a whole supermarket."

Elisa laughed. "Well, this refrigerator has everything a supermarket would have in it." I glanced at
the refrigerator. It was full of goodies. I still wasn't
hungry.

I watched Elisa making her sandwich. She was
going all out on it. There was ham, cheese, and every
kind of cold cut you could imagine.

"Sure you don't want something to eat, Kari?" she
asked.

Nothing could give me an appetite now. I was
waiting for Ripper to arrive. But when he came, what
would he do? Would he kill us both?

I tried to watch television, but I kept glancing toward the door. Elisa came over and sat down. I looked at her sandwich. It looked almost a foot high.

"Wish I could do this every night," she said.

I sure didn't feel that way. This might be my last night. Just then the phone rang. I jumped sky-high.

Elisa laughed. "What's the matter with you, anyway?"

"Should we answer it?" I asked.

"Are you kidding? Of course! Answer the phone. Don't be stupid."

The phone was right beside me. I wondered who it could be. Ripper?

As I lifted the receiver, I noticed my hand. It was shaking. I put the receiver to my ear and said, "Hello."

It was Paco. "Is Ripper there yet?"

"No, he's not here yet, Paco," I replied. I looked over at Elisa. She was staring right back at me. I'd better make up a story. "No, your cousin hasn't been here yet," I said into the phone.

Elisa turned back to the TV.

Paco said, "Listen, you stupid girl. I said Ripper was coming, not my cousin. Do you hear me?"

I didn't want Elisa alarmed. I said, "Sure enough, Paco. I understand you very clearly."

"Then get your story straight, will you?" he yelled.

Just then there was a knock on the door. The receiver dropped out of my hand. I knew who it was. Ripper!

I quickly picked up the receiver and said, "Someone knocked on your door."

"It's him," Paco said. "Now do your thing and stay cool." I put down the receiver and looked at Elisa.

She said, "Who do you think that is?" I saw the look on Elisa's face. She looked scared.

I was scared, too. Was Ripper going to kill us?

8

I held my breath. Ripper would come through that door any minute now. Would he slash me with his hook? I started toward the door. Elisa yelled. "Hold it, Kari. Something's wrong."

"Oh, it's probably just a friend of Paco's," I told her.

"Don't open that door." Elisa could sense trouble.

Now I was in a jam. I'd have to lie. "I'm expecting Paco's cousin," I said. "We'll use the back bedroom. He's going to pay lots of money."

"Are you sure?"

"Yeah, that's what Paco and I were just talking about. The guy will pay a thousand dollars."

"I thought we were supposed to have a night off," Elisa pouted. "That dirty Paco. He tricked us."

"We can't do anything about it now," I said. "A thousand dollars is a thousand dollars." I turned back to the door. "And put on a smile," I told Elisa.

Elisa gave a big grin. I knew she wasn't serious, but I wondered what she would do when she saw Ripper.

When I opened the door, I couldn't believe my

eyes! There stood Ripper and two other guys. They all looked mean.

"What are you doing here, Ripper?" I demanded.

He didn't answer, but barged right in, yelling, "Okay, girls, don't try anything smart. Both of you over on that lounge. Sit down and shut up!"

Ripper pointed his hook at me, and I jumped back. I didn't have to wait for him to tell me again. Elisa and I hurried over to the lounge and sat down. Elisa's eyes were as big as saucers. She was scared to death. I was too.

Ripper swaggered over. I looked up at him. He pointed his hook at my nose. "All right, where are the drugs?"

What was he talking about? I said, "Listen, Ripper, Elisa and I are here because we got a night off. That's all. We don't know anything."

Ripper grabbed me with his one good hand. He wore a ring shaped like a scorpion, encrusted with big diamonds. I looked up into his face. "You don't know where the drugs are?" he snarled.

I shook my head. Elisa was shaking her head, too. And that was the truth. I didn't know where any drugs were.

"Let's check this place out," Ripper barked to his companions. The two guys headed toward the bedroom. Soon they came out with Paco's clothes. One of them started ripping them.

"Hey, man, don't do that," I protested. "Those are Paco's clothes!"

The guy laughed. "Listen, little girl. I've been

around. Paco might have sewn his dope into the sleeves of these suits." They kept on ripping.

Then they started overturning chairs and ripping other things apart. Paco would arrive any moment now, and he'd probably start shooting. We were going to be in the middle of it. The thought made my stomach turn.

One guy came out from the bedroom. "Look what I found!"

My heart hit my throat. I hoped he hadn't found any drugs. Ripper would probably kill me for trying to cover up.

The guy held out his hand. In it were all kinds of jewelry—rings and bracelets. I knew whose they were—Paco's.

"Well, at least we got these," the guy said.

"We want more than that garbage," Ripper grunted. "That dude's got a lot of cocaine around someplace."

All this time I was waiting for Paco. Where was he? He was supposed to be here by now. If he only knew what was happening to his apartment.

The guys kept breaking up the furniture. Next they went to the kitchen, and I heard a lot of crashing and banging. Glasses and dishes were breaking all over the place. After that it was the refrigerator. They pushed it over with a loud crash.

With all this noise, what must the neighbors have thought? I wondered if they'd call the cops.

Ripper stood over Elisa and me. "Are you girls sure you're telling the truth?" he demanded.

I nodded vehemently. "So help me, it's the truth. It's the truth." I did my best to sound convincing. I didn't want Ripper using that hook of his on me.

The guys finally stopped looking. They hadn't found anything. I felt relieved.

Ripper grabbed my arm with the hook, and I felt the needle point on the end of it. "Ouch," I protested.

"Okay, girl, come with me."

"Do what?" I asked numbly.

"You're mine, Kari. I've had my eye on you, and now I've got you."

Now I knew there would be an all-out war. Ripper was sure to get killed by Paco.

Elisa spoke up. "Hey, Ripper. Cool it, man. Paco's not going to like this."

"Oh, yeah? Well, you're coming, too."

Elisa started to back away. Ripper lashed out with his hook. The end of it caught Elisa's blouse and tore a jagged hole.

"Nobody talks back to me," Ripper snorted. "Now, come along and shut up!"

Both of us jumped to our feet. I wasn't about to challenge Ripper now. I knew he could finish me with one swing.

We marched down the hallway. But where was Paco?

Paco's apartment was on the second floor. We went out the back way through the emergency exit.

When we got to the back alley, I saw Paco's Rolls Royce. "Where's Paco?" I said, without thinking.

Ripper chuckled, an evil sound. "He's tied up in

the backseat. I saw him sitting here, waiting for me. I knew it was a trap, but I was too smart for him. Two of my guys grabbed him after I went upstairs. Paco's finished, baby. I've wrecked his apartment, and I'm taking over his stable."

So that was it. Paco had been caught. But what about me? I hoped I'd survive this one.

We crossed the street to Ripper's car. Ripper threw Elisa and me in the backseat. One of his thugs drove, and Ripper sat in front. The other thug sat in back with us.

We went to an ordinary-looking neighborhood and pulled up in front of the house. Ripper said, "Okay, girls, come on in. You're mine now."

I thought it was strange. Here this guy had all that money, and he lived in an ordinary house. Maybe he didn't want to arouse any suspicion.

We marched into the house. Ripper kept looking at me. Then he laughed. I knew what he was thinking.

"I have VD," I lied. I thought I knew what Ripper had in mind, and I didn't want that to happen.

"I'll find that out myself," Ripper leered. He pointed toward the bedroom. "Over there, girl."

I looked toward the front door, trying to gauge my chance to escape. One of the other guys blocked my way. "Do what the boss said."

There was no way out. I headed for the bedroom, with Ripper right behind.

Ripper was an animal. I tried to fight back the best I could, but he was too big. He got what he wanted in the end.

It was a disgusting experience. It's bad enough to get paid for it, but it's completely different to get raped. I would never forget this.

We went back out to the front room. "You two are going to work now," Ripper told Elisa and me. "Don't try anything funny. You're mine. Understand?"

Elisa was trembling. I was scared to death, too. I knew I had to escape to Paco. Paco would get Ripper. I knew he would kill him.

We went back to Sunset Boulevard. We pulled up to the curb, and Ripper pushed me out. "Remember, you belong to me." This wasn't my usual block. I saw a couple of other girls, but I didn't recognize them. But I knew why they were there. And I was sure they belonged to Ripper.

I kept looking around. Somehow, some way, I had to get to Paco.

Then a car drove up. I looked inside. There were three guys.

They stopped and looked at me. I guess my fear made me desperate. I jerked open the door and started screaming, "Take me out of here. Take me out of here! These pimps kidnapped me from my pimp, and they're going to kill me!"

I was in the front seat on one guy's lap before they knew what was happening. "Get out of here. Get out of here before you get killed!" I shrieked.

They were three younger guys, and I don't know whether they were soliciting or not, but all three of them had their mouths wide open.

"Let's get out of here before you get killed," I repeated. "They're going to shoot you. Get going!"

The boy behind the wheel stomped on the gas, and we went sailing down the street.

We'd gone about six blocks when I turned around and looked out the back window. So far there was no Ripper.

The boy in the backseat said, "Stop the car and throw that girl out. We don't want to get caught in any pimp wars."

The driver swerved over to the curb. They were dumping me! I grabbed one boy by the shirt and hung on. "Please don't do that to me," I begged. "They're going to kill me."

I was hoping that Ripper hadn't seen what was happening. If he had, I knew either he or one of his thugs would be after us.

By this time the car was stopped. Two of the guys were trying to push me out, but I was hanging onto the third guy's shirt, crying. "Don't do it. Don't do it! They'll kill me."

I tried my best to hang on, but they were too strong. They jerked at my arms and pulled me away from the other guy. Then they had me. I felt myself being thrown. I hit the sidewalk and rolled. I looked up. The car peeled out and was gone.

That's when I saw Ripper's car. He pulled up to the curb. I jumped up and started running for it. One of the guys with him yelled, "She's getting away!"

I bolted across the busy street. I saw a car coming. It was a brand new one. It almost looked like one of

the pimps', but I had to take my chance. I ran in front
of the car and held up my hands. I began to wave
frantically. I was hoping the driver would see me and
stop.

Suddenly there was a screech of tires. He had
stopped! I jerked open the passenger door and
jumped in. I looked at the guy. He wasn't a pimp.

"Quick, get out of here," I told him. "They're trying to kill me."

"What are you talking about," he demanded.

"A pimp is trying to kill me. A pimp is trying to kill
me!" As soon as he heard that, I felt the car lurch
forward. He must have known what pimps were.

We sped down the street. I looked back. Somehow
we had lost Ripper's car. "Turn the corner, quick," I
said. The tires squealed as we roared through the
turn. A few blocks later, I turned around and looked
again. There wasn't anybody following.

"Thanks, mister, you saved my life," I said.

"Are you a hooker?" the guy asked.

"No, I'm not a hooker," I lied. "I'm a secretary at
Paramount Studios."

"What in the world are you yelling about a pimp
for, then?" I was stumped. I might as well level with
the guy. He had saved my life, after all.

"Okay, I lied," I admitted. "I got caught between
two pimps. One kidnapped me from the other one,
and you just helped me escape."

He looked at me. "You want help?"

"Want help? Of course I want help. Those guys
want to kill me!"

"Let's go right down to the police," he said. "They will arrest those guys."

I didn't want that. If Paco and Ripper got arrested, they could get out of jail easily. Then both of them would come looking for me. I didn't want that to happen.

"Mister, I don't know who you are," I said, "but I'd like to thank you. Going to the cops won't solve the problem, though. I'd get killed for sure if I had those guys arrested."

"I might as well tell you who I am," my rescuer told me. "I'm Jeff Harrison. I'm a television reporter here in L.A."

I looked at him blankly. Was he telling me the truth? "Are you sure?" I asked suspiciously.

He laughed. "Yes, I'm sure. I know who I am."

"Then what in the world were you doing on Sunset Boulevard?" Maybe he was down there to pick up a girl. With this new car, he certainly must have enough money.

"To tell you the truth, I was doing some research," he explained. "We're planning a segment on pimps and prostitutes, and that's why I was there."

Now I didn't know whether to laugh or cry. "Well, you certainly got into the middle of a story," I told him. "My name is Kari, and I work for a pimp."

"What's his name?"

I didn't want to give either Paco's or Ripper's name, so I had to think of something quick. "I work for a pimp by the name of Canteen," I improvised.

"Canteen, huh? Do you think we could go back and talk to him?"

"Oh, you don't want to talk to Canteen," I told him. "They did a story on him a few years ago, and they made up a bunch of lies about him. They portrayed him as being mean and ornery, and a vicious killer. Canteen isn't like that at all, so now he refuses to do any interviews at all." I looked at Mr. Harrison. Would he believe me?

"That's a very good story, young lady," he drawled. "Tell me another one." This guy had been around. I had to think of something else.

"Listen, if you want to do a story, it'll cost you a little money," I said.

"Oh, yeah, how's that?" he asked.

"Well, just go out and pick up a girl. I don't know if you're married or not, but pay the girl fifty bucks and just talk to her. That way you can get some good material. You know what I mean?"

"I don't have to go out and do that. Besides, my wife would never go for it. How about you, though?"

"What do you mean, how about me? Are you going to pay me for a story?"

"Oh, I think you owe me something, Kari. Don't you?"

This guy probably wanted it without paying for it. I'd met a few guys like that. They think they can do you a favor. I started to get mad. "Okay, mister, if that's the way you feel, let me out right now," I spat.

"Hey, wait a minute. Here I was, driving down Sunset Boulevard, and all of a sudden I see this young lady step in front of my car. If I hadn't stopped, I would have run her over. I pick her up, and then I find out that a pimp is trying to kill her. I risked my life to save her, and I get nothing in return! Maybe I should have let you go."

He was right. I guess I did owe him something. "Have it your way," I said tiredly. "What do you want?"

"I'll ask you some questions, all right?"

"Go ahead," I told him.

He was silent for a minute. Then he said, "Listen, I'll do you a favor. I have an expense account. Let's go check into a hotel room. I'll pay for your room, and you can stay there. Then we can talk, okay?"

"Mister, let's not play games," I said. "I owe you one for saving my life. You can have it free."

He jerked his head back. "Hey, don't get me wrong! I have a beautiful wife waiting at home for me, and I have a little daughter who's four years old. I've been propositioned I don't know how many times, but I'm not that kind of person. Understand?"

I felt embarrassed. "I'm sorry," I told him. "That's the only life I know."

He smiled. "I know I can't convince you to get out of your life-style, but I want to tell you something. You can trust me. I promise."

We found a hotel and parked at the curb. When we went up to the desk, the guy wanted to know our names.

My companion got all befuddled. "My name is Jeff Harrison, but this young lady needs a room for the night. She's the only one that needs the room."

The guy behind the counter looked at me, and then back at Jeff. I started to laugh. Then the man behind the counter said, "We don't want any hookers in our hotel."

Jeff looked at me. "You've been here before?"

"No, I haven't. And if the guy mentions the word *hooker* again, I'll slap him silly!"

"Both of you get out of here right now, or I'll call the cops," the guy snapped. "I don't want any hooker in here."

Jeff grabbed my arm, and we headed for the front door. When we got to the sidewalk, he said, "Kari, you've got a big mouth. You almost got us into trouble! All I need is to have the cops come and bust both of us. I'd probably lose my job! Next time, let's do it differently."

"Then let's decide who I am," I suggested. "Am I your sister, your wife, or your mistress?"

"Well, for one thing, you're not my mistress. Let's just say you're my younger sister, okay?"

We tried another hotel. I wondered how we were going to make out at this one.

When we got to the desk, Jeff said, "I'd like to rent a room for one night for my sister."

The man looked at me. "She's kind of young look-ing," he said slowly.

I held my breath. If this guy accused me of being a hooker, I didn't know what I'd do.

Jeff said, "Look, it's not what you think it is. She's

my sister, and she needs a room for the night. I'm willing to pay, okay?"

The guy didn't say another word. He just pushed the registration form toward me. I filled it out, but when I got to the address, I didn't know what to do. "Jeff, what shall I put for an address?" I asked.

Jeff gasped. "Don't you know where you live?" The man behind the counter was staring at us. I was trapped.

"Do you want me to put my home address from Wyoming?" I asked. I was trying to think how I could get out of this one.

"Listen, you two," the man said. "Why don't you quit playing games with me. I've been around a long time, and I'm not dumb. Two seconds after you walked in, I knew what this young lady was. Sir, why don't you just slip me an extra ten, and you can have your room."

I looked at Jeff. He was beet red. "Don't get me wrong," he said. "I'm not that kind of guy."

The man pointed his finger at me. "And don't tell me she's not that kind of girl."

I felt myself getting mad again, but I didn't want to cause a commotion. "Jeff, do what he says," I ordered.

Jeff paid the extra ten dollars, and the problem was settled. The guy gave us the key to the room. As we started to walk away, he said, "Have a good night's sleep."

Jeff spun around. "Don't get cute, buster."

I winked at the guy behind the counter, and he winked back. Then I reached up and put my arm around Jeff. He started to pull away, and I said, "Come here, tiger."

The guy behind the counter started to laugh, and so did I. But Jeff didn't. I don't know whether he looked scared or was trying to remain serious, but it was funny.

We went up to the room. I half expected Jeff to make an approach, but he just took out a note pad and pencil. He began asking me questions about my life.

At one point, I couldn't take it anymore. I broke down and cried. I felt so alone, filthy and dirty. There just had to be a different life from this.

Jeff tried his best to help me, but I just couldn't go back home, ever. My stepfather would take advantage of me again.

But where was I to go? I had no one to turn to. Jeff mentioned a few places, but I knew they wouldn't understand my problem. Besides, Paco would find me. Or worse yet, Ripper might.

Jeff called room service to get us some food, but I wasn't hungry. Jeff ordered himself a sandwich.

It was after midnight when Jeff got ready to leave. He stood in the doorway and looked down at me. "Kari, I want you to know I really care about you," he said. "My advice is to get out of L.A. and go back home."

I knew I couldn't go home. There was no way out

for me. I felt my eyes water. Then a tear rolled down my cheek. I looked up into Jeff's face. He seemed like the big brother I'd always wanted. I noticed he was getting teary eyed, too.

He reached out with his two big arms and put them around me. He squeezed me tight and said, "Kari, I wish you were really my sister. You seem to be the kind that would be great to have around."

There was a big lump in my throat. I didn't want to cry anymore.

Jeff touched my cheek. Then he took me under the chin and tilted my face up. "I love you like my very own sister," he told me.

I burst out crying. No one had ever told me that. Suddenly I felt so close to Jeff. Would it ever be possible to experience that brotherly kind of love? I knew it would never happen to me.

Jeff said, "I have to go now. I'll call tomorrow and see how you're doing."

"Jeff, I appreciate all that you've done," I said. "You saved my life. Is there anything I can do to pay you back?"

Jeff shook his head. Then he squeezed me again. *Could there be real love in this world?* I wondered.

Jeff turned and walked down the hall. I stood watching him go.

When he got to the elevator, he turned and waved, and I waved back.

The elevator doors opened, and he stepped inside. Then he was gone.

I stepped back and closed the door. I felt abandoned and terribly alone in that hotel room.

I would spend the night, but tomorrow I had to go. I must find Paco.

But when I went to find Paco, would Ripper get me first?

9

Much to my amazement, I slept soundly that night. It was mid-morning when I awoke.

The first thing I thought about was Paco. Would anybody come by and get him out of his car, or would he just die there, all tied up?

This could be my chance to get out of L.A. But if I took off, where would I go? No matter where I went, I'd probably end up the same way—on the streets with another pimp. I had no place to go but back to Paco.

I got out of bed and started dressing. Then the thought hit me. Maybe this was a setup. Maybe Jeff was another pimp. You never could trust a guy, I reasoned. I finished dressing and started for the door.

Just then the phone rang. I stopped and looked at it. Why would anybody be calling me? Nobody knew I was here, except Jeff Harrison and the guy down at the desk.

I had better answer, I decided. When I picked up the phone, I immediately recognized the voice at the other end. It was Jeff Harrison.

"How are you doing?" he asked.

"All right," I told him. I didn't want to tell him I was heading back to Paco.

"Have you had breakfast?"

"No, I'm just lying in bed, wondering what to do," I lied.

"Well, just stay there. I'll be right over. We can have breakfast together."

Before I had a chance to say anything else, he hung up. I ran to the door. I didn't want him to catch me here. I knew he'd never understand about Paco. I just wasn't ready to put my trust in anybody—not Paco, not Ripper, and not Jeff. I had to keep my eyes open and be careful.

Outside the hotel, I hailed a taxi. I got in and told the driver where I wanted to go. Now I had to figure out how to pay him. It was a good thing he didn't ask for the money first, because I was flat broke.

When we got to Paco's car, I said, "Mister, my friend is tied up in that car. Let me untie him, and I'll get you the money."

The cabby reached over the seat and grabbed my arm. "I've heard all the excuses in the book, kid. Pay me now, or I'm calling the cops."

I didn't want that. I said, "Mister, you've got to believe me. My friend is over in that Rolls Royce, tied up. I've got to help him."

"Don't get smart with me," he said. "Just give me the money. You owe me eight bucks, not counting the tip."

"Can't you see I don't even have a purse," I yelled.

"I don't have any money on me! I'm not trying to trick you or anything. I'll get you your money as soon as we untie my friend. You can come with me. I won't try anything."

The cabby stared at me for a couple of seconds. Then he let go of my shoulder. "All right, let's go look." We got out of the car. "I used to be a track star at U.S.C.," he warned. "If you make a run for it, kid, I'll catch you before you get ten feet away."

"Oh, can it," I snapped. He was getting on my nerves by now.

He grabbed my arm again. "Don't get smart with me! You owe me money. If your friend isn't in that car, we're going to the cops, and they're going to put you away. Do you hear?"

I shrugged my shoulders and sauntered across the street.

When we got to the car, I looked in the backseat. There was Paco, motionless. His hands and feet were tied, and he was gagged.

I yanked open the door and shook him. Paco's eyes fluttered open, then widened. I knew he was surprised to see me. I quickly took the gag out of his mouth.

Paco's first words were, "I'll kill him. I'll kill him!" The taxi driver started backing up. He must've thought Paco meant him.

"Don't worry, he's not mad at you," I reassured him.

"Untie me, would you?" Paco growled. I tried, but the knots were too tight.

"Mister, give me a hand, will you?" I said over my shoulder.

The cabby pulled a switchblade out of his pocket. I took it and cut the ropes around Paco's wrists and ankles. He hobbled out of the backseat and began to curse. "So help me, it's all over for that guy." The taxi driver started backing up again.

"Paco, you have to pay for the cab," I said. "I owe eight bucks."

"How'd you get here?" Paco asked.

"I'll tell you about it later. Just pay the driver. I don't have any money."

Paco reached in his pocket and peeled a twenty-dollar bill off his roll. "Keep the change," he said, handing it to the cabby.

At the sight of the money, a change came over the taxi driver. He pocketed the twenty and then said, "My special taxi price is fifty dollars."

"What are you talking about?" Paco demanded.

"Listen, I had to risk my life to bring this girl here. Besides, if I hadn't brought her, you would have died in that backseat. I call that emergency care. If it wasn't for me, you'd be dead, man."

I was furious. I don't mind paying what I owe, but this was a rip-off! "Mister, you'd better get out of here while you can," I told him. The cabby didn't move.

"Maybe you want me to cut you?" I asked. I flicked open the switchblade he'd given me a few minutes before.

The knife persuaded him. He started back toward

his cab. "And you can forget what you saw here," I called after him. He drove off.

Paco and I got in the Rolls and headed out of there. As we drove, Paco was massaging his wrists. "So help me, I tried everything in that backseat. I tried tapping on the window, groaning, and kicking. Nothing happened. All night I wondered if anyone would ever come."

"You think you had problems," I said. "Ripper almost killed me!"

"I'm sorry, Kari. That's not the way I planned it. That Ripper is smarter than I thought."

"Ripper raped me. Then he put me out on the street to work for him. I was lucky to escape."

"I thought I had him figured out, Kari. When he pulled up, I waited until he got inside the building. Then I started after him. But I didn't know Ripper had two of his goons outside. They came up behind me and pulled a gun. At first they wanted to kill me, but they decided to let me rot in my own car."

"Why didn't they just kill you?" I wanted to know.

"I'm worth more to Ripper alive than dead," Paco said.

"What are you talking about?"

"I know what Ripper's up to. He's after my cocaine, but I'm too smart to leave it where he can find it."

"Well, wherever you're hiding it, it's a good place," I said. "Ripper and his bunch tore that apartment to pieces, but all they found was some of your jewelry."

"I'll tell you something," Paco smiled. "If they'd found the cocaine, they probably would have killed me. Since they didn't, they'll keep me alive to see if I'll lead them to it. But that'll never happen."

I felt an urge to ask Paco where his cocaine was. After all, I had rescued him from death. I looked over at him as he drove. I'd better not ask, I decided. If I knew too much, he might kill me someday.

"I'm going to get Ripper," Paco said.

"I hope you do. He's after me, too. I'd feel a lot better if you'd get him first!"

We drove to the mansion. One of the butlers met us at the door and said, "Mr. Paco, the police have been here with a search warrant. They almost tore the place apart! I don't know what they were after."

Paco hurried through the door. I followed him into the house. I couldn't believe it! Furniture was everywhere. It didn't take me long to figure out what they were after—cocaine.

Paco must be a very big cocaine dealer. Cocaine was undoubtedly a bigger income for him than his girls. But why do both? Maybe someday I'd find out.

Paco went from room to room. The butler and I followed him. Paco was swearing about the big mess.

He turned to the butler. "Did any of them search around the swimming pool?"

"Yes, they looked everywhere, sir, even under the tiles by the swimming pool."

"Did any of them go into the pool?" Paco asked.

"No, sir. Nobody went into the pool. They all had their clothes on. Nobody seemed to want to swim."

Somehow, Paco's cocaine had something to do with that swimming pool. I wondered what.

Paco said, "Kari, we've got to move the operation into the city. I want you to pack up your things. Then we'll tell the girls along the Strip what's happening. The only person that's going to stay here is my butler."

As I was packing my things, I heard something that sounded like a splash. I went to the window and looked out. There was Paco in the swimming pool. That was strange.

Paco went under the water. Why was he doing that? I watched. He was down there awhile. When he surfaced, he looked around. I slipped behind the bedroom curtain. Evidently he didn't see me. He dove again. In a few seconds he came up, holding a rather large boxlike thing. It was wrapped in plastic. He swam to the edge and jumped out.

Paco hurried into the house. Then I knew the answer. Paco hid his cocaine at the bottom of the pool. He must have a secret compartment down there. Very smart.

Paco was waiting when I got downstairs. I didn't want to say anything about his being in the swimming pool. If he knew that I knew, he might easily kill me. I would never tell anybody about that secret compartment.

We got back in the car and went to the Strip. Paco said, "I've got to make a contact now. Be right back. You wait here."

I got out of the car. I didn't know whether Paco

wanted me to turn a trick or what. "You want me to work?" I asked.

"No, don't work. Just wait for me here. I won't be long."

Paco drove off. I looked around. There were a couple of girls on the street. I thought about Ripper. What would I do if Ripper came by? I backed up and stepped inside the doorway of a building. I hoped nobody would see me there.

Paco must have gone to stash his cocaine. I wondered where he'd put it now. Maybe he'd put it in a safe-deposit box. But couldn't the cops get into those?

I must have waited a half hour. Cars kept driving by. In fact, one guy thought I was working and tried to proposition me. I told him I was a cop. He took off in a hurry. I laughed as he sped away. But inside, I was scared. Would the next car be Ripper's?

Finally I saw Paco's Rolls. He pulled up to the curb, and I jumped in. "Everything okay?" I asked.

"Yeah, I think so. But I have another job to do, and I need your help."

"What kind of job?" I wondered if it had something to do with his cocaine.

"I have to teach Ripper a lesson," Paco replied. "He thought it was smart to keep me alive, but he's going to regret it."

This was a full-scale pimp war. Paco had already killed Cowboy. Now was he going to kill Ripper? I didn't want anything to do with it. "Don't you think I'd better get on the street and start working?" I asked. "We could probably use some money."

"No, Kari. I don't want you to do that," Paco said. "I need to use you to get back at Ripper."

"Paco, I don't want to be difficult or anything like that, but as soon as Ripper sees me, he'll try to kill me. He chased me down the street when I ran for it. I didn't tell you this, but a TV reporter picked me up and took me to a hotel. That's where I was last night. I'm sure Ripper hasn't forgotten about it, though. He's after me!"

"Well, he probably only wants you to be part of his stable, but we're going to set him up. I'm going to teach him a little lesson. Then you won't need to worry about him anymore."

"Are you going to kill him?" I asked.

"Let's just say I'm going to teach him a lesson. Now, come on."

I knew there was no sense in arguing with Paco. He might get mad and do me in. I'd better do what he wanted.

We drove a few more blocks. Then Paco said, "I see Ripper standing on that street corner. His car's just a few feet from him. When he sees you, he'll probably grab you, throw you in the car, and take off. He'll try to take you to his place, but that's when I'm going to get him."

This didn't sound too good. We had tried to set Ripper up before. Last time, Ripper had gotten me and Paco both.

"Why don't you just take your gun and shoot him," I suggested. "Pull the trigger and blow his brains out!"

"That'd be too easy. He wanted me to die in my own car."

"Are you going to do that to him?"

"You ask too many questions, Kari." I could tell Paco was getting mad. I'd better shut up.

We pulled around the corner. "All right, this is what I want you to do," Paco said. "You're going to walk right by Ripper. But before you do, I want to be down at the other end of the block. I'll give you a wave when it's time to walk toward Ripper. As soon as he sees you, he'll probably try to grab you. Turn around and run a little bit. But make sure he catches you."

"Paco, he'll grab me with his hook," I protested. "You know he can rip people apart."

"Don't worry about that. Just do what I say, and I promise he won't slash you."

This was going to be interesting. How could Paco promise me that?

"When he starts chasing you, just stop and turn around," Paco went on. "Then grab your dress and pull it up."

"Do what?" I wasn't sure I'd heard right.

"I said, just before he grabs you, take your dress and pull it up."

"That's embarrassing," I protested. "I can't do that."

"It's called shock," Paco explained, "just plain old shock. When you do that, he'll stop. Then you tell him you'll do whatever he wants."

"Are you sure this is going to work?"

"Kari, it works, believe me. It's so unexpected, you throw the other person off balance. One of the girls did it to a cop once, and the cop got so flustered, he let her go. It's a sure thing."

I thought about it. Paco was right. I knew it was going to be a little embarrassing, but I hoped it would shock Ripper. As long as it stopped that hook from slicing me!

We got out of the car. Paco said, "Now remember. Watch for me. When I wave, it's time for you to start walking toward Ripper. And do just as I said. When he takes you to the car, agree to whatever he wants. If he says you have to work for him for thirty years, tell him you will. All you have to do is go along with him. I'll take care of it from there."

"What are you going to do?" I asked.

"Just leave it to me. There's no way he can trick me on this one."

"But, Paco. Suppose he has some of his guys down the block? They got you before. Maybe they'll get you again."

The way Paco explained it, it sounded so simple. I knew something could go wrong. Maybe pulling up my dress wouldn't work. Maybe they would grab Paco from behind. And maybe Ripper would kill me right on the street.

Paco said, "I'll be watching. You can count on that."

"Maybe you could disguise yourself," I suggested. "Then Ripper wouldn't see you coming, and you could kill him right there."

"Don't be silly, Kari. The only way I'm going to get Ripper into his car is by using you. I'll teach him a lesson that he'll never forget. Nothing will go wrong."

"I'm absolutely scared to death," I confessed.

"Listen, it's either you or him. It's either him or me. When you think about it that way, you're not afraid of death. You overcome fear of death by realizing the other guy is going to kill you, just as in war. If you don't shoot him first, you're dead. Now, Kari, if we don't get Ripper, Ripper will get us both. Understand?"

I understood, but I was still afraid. I knew something could go wrong. And if it did, that would be the end of me—especially if Ripper realized I was setting him up.

"Now let me repeat your instructions," Paco said. "Timing is important on this. Don't approach Ripper until you see me wave. I'll be watching everything you do, and as soon as he heads toward you, I'll make my move. You got it?"

"You want me to wait until I see you wave at me. When you wave, I'm supposed to walk toward Ripper."

"That's right. Wait for the wave."

Then I had a sudden fear. "What if Ripper doesn't come toward me," I asked. "Suppose he just ignores me. What then?"

Paco laughed. "Pimps don't have short memories, Kari. It all happened just last night. As soon as Ripper sees you, he'll go crazy. You won't have to pretend you're running, babe!"

That really scared me. I wished he hadn't said that. Paco said, "Don't worry. Everything's going to be okay."

No amount of reassurance would cause me not to worry. That's what he had tried to tell me the last time. I knew I was facing a life-or-death situation. I hoped I would make it. But I wasn't sure.

10

I couldn't believe I was doing this. It seemed like an easy way to get myself killed.

Ripper was staring down the street, his back to me. I had to be careful that he didn't catch sight of me too soon. I didn't want to mess Paco up.

Sitting in front of Ripper was his car, a beautiful white Rolls Royce. It must have cost way over a hundred thousand dollars. He had probably paid for it in cash, too. My thoughts were interrupted by the signal. Paco had been peering cautiously around the corner of a building down the street, and now he moved his hand.

This was it. I started walking toward Ripper. I hoped he'd look my way pretty soon. I didn't want to get too close.

Ripper was staring at the pavement, oblivious to me. I certainly wasn't going to walk up to him and say hello. I stopped and called, "Hey, Ripper!"

He jerked up his head and stared at me. Then his features contorted, and he came toward me, flexing his hook. I started backing up.

"Come here, you tramp!" he grated. "You're mine. Don't you try to run this time. If you pull anything, I'll kill you."

I kept backing up. "Stop," Ripper commanded. "Don't you take another step."

Down the block, Paco was creeping toward us, staying close to the buildings. Was he going to jump Ripper from behind?

"Stop right there," Ripper hollered. I kept backing up. Ripper had a vicious look in his eyes. I knew he was boiling mad.

Ripper sped up. I was backing up as fast as I could go. I didn't want to turn around and have him get me from behind. I made sure he was facing me.

Ripper was almost on me now, and he was getting ready to grab me. Then I remembered what Paco had told me. I grabbed the skirt of my dress and pulled it up. Would it work?

I peeked over the top of my dress. Ripper had stopped. His mouth was open. "Why did you do that?" he asked.

"I just wanted you to take a look, that's all." Paco had been right. Ripper was in shock.

"Why did you run away from me?" Ripper asked, stepping up to me.

"Man, I've been around. Paco used to beat me severely," I lied. "I don't know how many times I was left for dead. So I didn't want another pimp getting me. That's why I had to run from you." I hoped he was swallowing this.

Ripper threw his good arm around my neck. Then

he pushed his hook under my nose. "Now I've got you," he snarled.

"Listen, Ripper, let's talk this over, man," I pleaded.

Where was Paco? I glanced up the street. He was nowhere in sight.

Ripper started dragging me toward his car. "Okay, kid, we're going to get in my car and talk a little bit. After we get through talking, I'm going to teach you a lesson or two."

I didn't know whether to scream or what. If I screamed, maybe I'd attract the cops. We'd probably both go to jail then.

Ripper dragged me to the car and pulled open the door. He stepped in first, then pulled me inside. "Slam the door, kid."

He had me by the hair. I tried to pull my head forward, but he held it tight. "Loosen up a little, would you?" I said.

"Loosen nothing, baby. Here, take this." Ripper pulled my hair hard. It felt as if my hair was pulling out. I gasped in pain, but I somehow managed to shut the door. Ripper jerked me down beside him. Then he took his hook, dug it into my dress, and twisted it around. "You won't get away from me this time!"

He started up the car. "Where are you taking me?" I demanded.

"I'm taking you back to my house. Little girls like you have to be taught a lesson."

"But what are you going to do to me?" I was

scared. "Don't hurt me, Ripper. Please don't hurt me."

"Don't worry, Kari. First, I'll tie you up for a few days without any food. Then I'll beat you a few times. After that, you'll do whatever I say."

I didn't want that to happen. I said, "Ripper, you don't want to do that to me. I can make lots of money on the street. I made thousands of dollars for Paco. Put me on the street, and I'll make you rich. I promise I'll never leave you, never again. I'll never run away again."

"You'd better believe you won't," Ripper snapped.

We drove four or five blocks. I knew Ripper was going to beat me, just like the other pimps. They beat you to scare you, so you won't run away. But I knew Paco was close behind. At least I hoped so. I hoped Ripper's bodyguards hadn't grabbed him this time. If they had, I knew it was all over for me.

I looked over at Ripper. And then I saw something. Paco was in the backseat, and he was slowly getting up. He had a switchblade in his hand. I smiled at him. Ripper noticed. "What are you laughing about?"

This was going to be fun. I said, "You sure are a big, fat slob!"

Ripper's eyes widened in disbelief. Then he twisted my dress some more. "Nobody talks to me that way. Who do you think you are, anyway?"

In the backseat, Paco had a big smile on his face. I knew he was ready to burst out laughing.

"I ought to steal all your jewelry," I taunted Ripper. "What kind of jerk are you, anyway, wearing all those diamonds?"

Ripper got so red, I thought he would explode. "No woman talks to me that way," he shrieked. "You're as good as dead, you hear me? I'm going to tear you to pieces! You'll wish you were never born before I'm through with you."

"You don't have the guts to do something like that," I flung back at him. I'm sure Ripper couldn't believe what he was hearing. I felt so thrilled by what I was saying, knowing that Paco was in the backseat with his switchblade.

I stole a glance at Paco. He had his hand over his mouth. I'm sure he thought this was the funniest thing he had ever seen.

"Ripper, what I ought to do is to kill you," I went on. "It would make a lot of girls happy if you were dead."

Ripper slammed on the brakes and swerved over to the side of the road. He was livid with rage. "I'm not taking you to my house," he screamed. "I'm killing you right now!"

"That's what you think," Paco said quietly, as he grabbed Ripper's hair with one hand. He pulled Ripper's head back and stuck the point of the switchblade in the soft spot right under the chin.

"Who's that?" Ripper gasped.

"That's a policeman," I told him, "a real, live L.A.P.D. detective. I set you up, sucker. He's arresting you, but first we're going to rip you off. Isn't that funny?"

Ripper reached up with his good hand. Paco yelled, "Put your hand down, Ripper, or I'll saw your head off with this switchblade. Put it down to your side, and don't you dare move!"

Ripper's eyes were bugging out of his head. He looked so grotesque. I wondered what Paco would do next.

"Well, shall I take his jewelry?" I asked. "He's got some expensive things."

"Yeah, Kari, take his jewelry." I reached over to grab Ripper's good hand, but he clenched his fist. I tried to pry his fingers open.

"Nobody takes my diamonds and gets away with it," he said. "Get your filthy hands off me, Kari."

"Don't give us a bad time, Ripper," Paco warned. I kept pulling on Ripper's clenched fist. "He won't open his hand," I said.

"Well, let's see if his blood is red, then." Paco took a little jerk with his knife. Ripper screamed. Then I saw a spurt of blood. Ripper began to swear, but wouldn't open his fist. I looked at Paco and shrugged. Paco said, "Show Ripper what's happening underneath his chin."

I took some of the blood and put my finger right in front of Ripper's face. Paco said, "Open your hand and quit resisting, Ripper, or the next time it'll be a stream of blood."

Ripper's hand relaxed. I jerked the ring from his hand and looked at it. It was the scorpion with loads of diamonds. It looked hideous, but expensive.

"Take his diamond bracelet, too," Paco ordered. I

unsnapped the bracelet. Ripper had diamonds all over the place. I knew this bracelet must be worth thousands.

"Get his watch, too, Kari," Paco said. The watch was encrusted with diamonds, too.

"Any other diamonds?" Paco asked. There was another ring, which I took. Then I looked around Ripper's neck. There were more diamonds there. I took them all.

Paco reached out his free hand. I put the stuff in his hand, and he jammed it all in his pocket. I was hoping that later Paco would share this expensive jewelry with me.

Then Paco said, "Okay, Ripper. I'm going to ease up a little on the blade. Drive, and do what I say."

"Tell him to take his hook off my dress, too," I said. I didn't have to wait for an answer from Paco. Ripper immediately freed me. I knew he was really scared now.

"What are you going to do with me?" Ripper asked.

"You're going to jail," Paco replied. Ripper turned around to plead with him, and then saw who it was.

"Paco! Man, you had me going there. Listen, you can have your girl Kari. I didn't mean any harm, okay?"

Paco jabbed the pointed blade into the side of Ripper's cheek. Blood spurted. Ripper screamed. "Please man, don't you understand? Let's talk about this. Don't hurt me any more."

Paco's voice was cold. "Ripper, I have your jewelry, and the only thing you have left is your life. Do what I say, or I'll take that, too."

"Okay, have it your way. But, listen, you can have Kari back. If that doesn't satisfy you, I'll give you another one of my girls. What do you say?"

"Just shut up and drive," Paco said. "I'll tell you where to go." I thought about what Paco had done to Cowboy. Was he going to do the same thing? I didn't want to witness another murder.

We pulled out from the curb. I knew I was in danger, too. Would Paco kill me as well as Ripper?

"Ripper, what did you do to my apartment?" Paco asked.

Ripper stared straight ahead. Paco grabbed the back of his hair again and jerked on it. Then he put the switchblade to Ripper's neck. "I said, what did you do to my apartment?"

Ripper said, "I didn't do a thing, absolutely nothing."

"Don't lie to me, Ripper. What did you do, and what did you take?"

"I told you, I didn't take anything," he yelled.

"Ripper, you're a dirty, filthy liar," I cut in. "I saw what you did. You tore the place apart. You and your men ripped it to pieces."

"Ripper, is that what happened to it?" Paco demanded.

"Why don't we go back and take a look?" Ripper asked. "Then you'll see for yourself. Your apartment has not been touched."

"What did you do to my apartment?" Paco repeated.

"Listen, I just went up there to check it out. I was looking for an apartment. My house is just an ordinary house, and I got a little bit of money, so I wanted to get an apartment. Then I ran into Kari, and she said she wanted to leave you. She asked to come with me, and I told her no. You know how it is, Paco. I'm not about to steal your girl."

I exploded. That weasel Ripper was lying! "I'll tell you what he was doing, Paco. He was up there, stealing all your jewelry. After that, he tore the place apart. He was looking for drugs. That's what he was doing, looking for drugs."

"Is that what you were looking for, Ripper?" Paco asked.

"This girl is lying to you," Ripper protested. "She's lying. You know these girls. They would lie to anybody. They lie to their johns, to their pimps. They lie to their parents. They lie to the cops. She's just lying."

"Ripper also tried to kidnap me," I said. "You know about that one, Paco."

"Okay, Ripper, suppose you didn't do anything to my apartment," Paco said. "Two of your men grabbed me, tied me up, and left me in my car. What do you say about that?"

"I don't know anything about your car. If somebody tied you up in a car, I had nothing to do with it. Absolutely nothing."

"He's lying, Paco," I yelled.

Paco sat there, staring straight ahead. I wondered what he was thinking. It was probably how to get rid of Ripper. It could be bloody.

Paco directed Ripper onto the freeway, and we headed toward downtown L.A. We got off the freeway and drove through the heart of the city. We seemed to be heading toward the place where Paco had disposed of Cowboy.

Blood was still seeping from the wound on Ripper's chin. It was running down onto his shirt. He looked a horrible mess. I hoped that nobody would see us and call the cops.

Then we got to the rough section of town. Again there were dilapidated old buildings and vacant warehouses. I knew we were in the same area where Cowboy had gotten it. And I knew what was going to happen. Ripper was going to get killed.

Ripper must have sensed it. "Paco, let's stop and talk this over," he suggested. "Just tell me your price, and I'll give it to you, okay?"

"We're not discussing money now, Ripper. You did me in, man. You did me in bad. You thought you could leave me in that car of mine to rot. You hoped I'd croak, didn't you?"

"You've got me wrong, all wrong," Ripper protested. "I don't know anything about that. All I know is, I went to an apartment to check it out. That's all I know!"

It surprised me how pimps would lie. But I guess I really shouldn't be surprised. I knew Ripper was fighting for his life.

"Turn to the right here," Paco said. Ripper wasn't slowing down. Paco screamed. "I said, turn right!"

Ripper put on the brakes, hard. We pitched forward, and Paco said, "One more cute little trick like that, and I'll cut your head right off!"

Ripper didn't say anything. I looked at him. His eyes were darting back and forth. Of all things, he was probably looking for a cop.

We drove a few more blocks. Beads of sweat formed on Ripper's forehead. "Listen, Paco," he whined, "don't act this way. You taught me a lesson already. You stabbed me in the neck, and I'm bleeding. You took my jewelry. If you want more money, I'll get it for you. Just tell me what you want. Talk to me, won't you? Please talk to me."

I looked at Paco. His face was hard.

Ripper went on, "Listen, let's go to my bank. I have a million dollars there. I'll give you a million in cash. What do you say?"

"That's not enough. I want a hundred million."

No way would Ripper have that kind of money. I waited for his answer.

"Listen, you can have your hundred million," Ripper blurted out. "Go back to my bank, and I'll give you a hundred million dollars in cash. You can have it in thousand-dollar bills, or any way you want it, I swear."

Now I knew Ripper was fighting for his life. Certainly he didn't have a hundred million dollars in cash. No pimp would have that amount of money. I knew Ripper was trying to buy time. Maybe some of

his men would see what was happening and shoot
Paco. But I knew it was too late for Ripper now.

Paco said, "Turn left here." I recognized the building to my right. It was the place where Cowboy was
shot. I thought maybe Paco would have Ripper stop
there, but we drove on.

We went about six blocks farther. Then we turned
right. A couple of blocks later we turned left again.

"Pull over to the side here," Paco ordered. Ripper
pulled over, and we sat there in silence. I looked at
Ripper. His eyes were darting back and forth again.
By this time he was sweating profusely.

Paco said, "Ripper, you've been a bad man, a very
bad man."

Much to my surprise, Ripper said, "Yes, I've been
a very bad man."

"You deserve to die, then," Paco said.

"Yes, I deserve to die," Ripper repeated. "I'm a
very bad man."

It sounded as though Ripper was delirious. Was he
putting on a big act? I knew he couldn't be trusted.

Ripper said, "Paco, let me have one more chance.
Let's work a deal, huh?"

"How come you didn't work a deal with me when I
was back in my car, dying, man? That was the longest
night I've ever spent. I was gagged and bound, and
you didn't care. Did you?"

"Okay" Ripper sighed. "I'll be straight with you. It
was my men who tied you up, and I did go to your
apartment. Yeah, I was looking for drugs. You and I
both know that you're one of the biggest dealers

around. I was just trying to get some drugs. But I didn't find any. Now let me pay for the damages to your apartment, and let's call it square. Okay?"

Paco lost his temper. "You're a filthy liar, aren't you, Ripper? You'd kill your own mother, wouldn't you?" Ripper sat there, staring straight ahead. "And how many people have you killed?" Paco said.

Ripper didn't answer. "Since you're being so honest, how many people have you killed?" Paco repeated.

"It's none of your business what I do, Paco," Ripper flared. "Put your blade away, and let's get out of here. I'll pay you what you want."

"It's not that easy," Paco yelled. "You tried to kill me, like all the other people you've killed! You deserve to die." He turned to me. "Kari, step outside, please."

It was coming. Paco was going to kill Ripper. I opened the door. Ripper yelled, "Kari, do something! Convince Paco to let me go. I'll pay you well."

But I knew nothing would change Paco's mind. I silently got out of the car and closed the door behind me. I walked a few feet down the deserted street.

There was a scream, and then a horrible gurgling sound. I almost turned around to look, but then I stopped. I didn't want Paco to see me witness what was happening.

In a few minutes I heard the car door open. Then Paco said, "Okay, Kari. Let's get out of here." I glanced back at the car.

"Don't look. Don't look!" Paco yelled, but it was

too late. I had already looked. Paco grabbed me by the arm and said, "Let's get out of here."

"But what about the car and the body?" I asked.

"I'm sorry I had to do that to Ripper. If I hadn't, he would have killed me. I know about Ripper. Nobody would take him that far without getting killed. If I had let him go, I would have signed my own death warrant. I'm sorry, Kari. It was crude the way I had to do it. But if I didn't do it, he would have killed me, and you, too."

I was still too stunned to say anything. At least we weren't getting back in the car.

We hurried down the street. Paco said, "I wanted to make sure Ripper died in his own car. He wanted me to die in mine."

We alternated between walking and running for a few blocks. I was all out of breath. Paco had me around the waist.

We finally got to where traffic was heavier. Paco said, "Here, take this."

I looked at it. It was Ripper's diamond bracelet.

Something inside made me feel sick to my stomach. There was no way I could accept that bracelet. It reminded me of Ripper's violent death.

"Thanks, Paco, but I can't take it," I said.

"Why not?" he asked.

I had to think of an excuse. "If I was out working the street and had that on my wrist, I'm afraid somebody might murder me and steal the bracelet," I said.

Paco took it back. He still wanted me as his slave—a worthless slave.

11

We walked a few more blocks and found a taxi. Paco directed the driver to the apartment.

When we walked through the door, some of the girls were busy putting things back in place, but most of the furniture was damaged.

Paco was really upset. He began to curse and said that death had been too good for Ripper. I still couldn't get that scene out of my mind. It was so gruesome. I never wanted to see anything like that again.

Then Paco began to laugh. "Well, they didn't get our dope, did they, girls?"

I wondered what Paco had done with the package of cocaine he'd pulled from the swimming pool. Where could he have hidden it?

That evening, Paco took the girls to the street, but he kept me back at the apartment. He told me to stay there until he got back. That really worried me.

To pass the time, I flicked on the television. There was a movie on about drug trafficking. It scared me, so I turned it off and sat there by myself, in complete silence. I had to sort things out in my head. I knew I had to get out of here. But, where would I go? There had to be someplace.

Maybe I knew too much about Paco. Would he try to kill me? If he'd kill Cowboy and Ripper, I knew he could easily kill me, too. I had better get out before it was too late.

That's when Paco came back. "C'mon," he told me. "We've got something to do."

It couldn't be prostitution. If it had been that, he would have taken me to the street with the other girls. "Where are we going?" I asked.

Paco glared at me. I knew I'd asked the wrong question. "That's none of your business," he spat. I knew I had better be careful from now on. Paco might shoot me in the head or slash my throat. I shuddered at the images that flashed through my mind.

"Sorry," I mumbled. "Whatever you say." That seemed to settle him down.

We went down to the street to get into the car. Just before he slipped behind the wheel, Paco looked in the backseat. I knew why. He was thinking about Ripper, and he didn't want anybody behind him, slashing his throat. I looked at the backseat on my side. Then we looked at each other. Paco shrugged his shoulders. "You can never be too sure."

I didn't say anything. Paco was really uptight about something. Where was he going to take me?

We got on the freeway and drove north along the coast. Then we came into Malibu.

Malibu is where a lot of the movie stars and people in the film industry live. I knew a lot of those people used drugs, and I suspected this trip involved something in the way of drugs.

Paco was too tense to make conversation, so we just rode in silence. We finally pulled into a restaurant along the waterfront. Maybe Paco was taking me out to eat.

"C'mon with me," Paco grunted. We walked inside. The maître d' met us at the door. I knew that Paco and I weren't just going out to dinner. I could tell that by the edge in his voice. What was going to happen?

The maître d' put us at a table next to the window and gave us menus. I looked at Paco. "Order what you want but make it snappy," he said tersely.

My mind went blank. I didn't really feel like eating now. The way Paco was acting made me nervous.

The waiter asked if we wanted a cocktail. "Don't drink," Paco grunted. The man left us. I knew that was a lie. Paco did too drink. At his place in Beverly Hills, he had lots of booze. I still couldn't figure him out.

"What do you want?" Paco asked.

The only thing I could think of was fried shrimp, so I blurted out, "Fried shrimp."

"I wonder how long that will take to cook," he said thoughtfully.

For the life of me, I didn't know. "Should I order something else?" I asked anxiously.

"No, that's okay for now." Paco kept looking

around. I started to look around, too. "Keep your eyes on the table, stupid!" he hissed. I buried myself in my menu. I started to shake. Maybe someone was going to try to shoot us right here in the restaurant!

I looked up at Paco again. He was still looking back and forth. His eyes met mine. I looked down at the menu again. He said, "If you keep looking around, stupid, people will think something is wrong."

Maybe this was the place Paco had hidden his dope. If the cops were looking for dope, they certainly wouldn't come to a restaurant like this. At least I didn't think so.

Paco looked at me. "Act like you're getting sick to your stomach," he said calmly.

"What did you say?" I couldn't believe my ears.

"Start vomiting, Kari. That's an order!"

"What did you say? Did you say to start vomiting?" Then, I felt something hit my foot. Paco was kicking me.

"Do it," he whispered.

The guy must be crazy. I stared at him and said, "Right here?"

"Act like you're going to get sick on the table. Right now!"

This had to be one of the most stupid things I had ever heard. But I had better do what he said. I pretended I was going to get sick on the table. Just then a waiter came by. "Something the matter?" he asked.

Paco jumped up. "Sorry, my wife is sick. She's

pregnant, and the slightest thing sets her stomach off."

I kept it up. I wondered what in the world was going on. But I had better play the part. Paco would beat me up later if I didn't do a good job.

"I'm sorry," Paco told the waiter. "This is very embarrassing. I've got to get her out into some fresh air."

All the people at the nearby tables had stopped eating and were staring at me. I felt terribly embarrassed.

Paco had a strong hand on my arm. He half pushed me out the door and into the parking lot. I couldn't help it. I blurted out, "What was that for?"

"I had to get out of there, but I didn't know how. I thought if you started to get sick, they wouldn't suspect anything. Come on, let's get out of here!"

I started to say something. Then I caught myself. I was going to ask Paco why he didn't just give the guy ten dollars and walk out. It seemed stupid to attract so much attention. At times I wondered about Paco. He didn't always use his head.

We got into the car, and Paco took off fast. He started swearing. "So help me, if Eric sets me up like that again, I'll kill him!"

Without thinking, I said, "Who's Eric?"

"It's Eric Armentani. He was supposed to be there. I know this is the place we were supposed to meet, and he was nowhere in sight!"

"Well, maybe something happened. Maybe he got a flat tire or something."

"Don't use excuses like that, Kari. That excuse went out with the hula hoop. I want to call that guy and find out what happened. If he stood me up, that'll be the last time he stands anybody up."

There was a phone booth in a parking lot ahead. Paco swerved over and stopped beside it. He jumped out.

I watched Paco dial a number. Then he became very agitated and angry. I couldn't hear what he was saying, but whoever he was talking to was getting an earful.

Paco slammed down the receiver and marched back to the car. He jumped in beside me. "Eric was afraid. He said there was a bunch of cops near that place. I didn't see any cops, did you?"

"No, but maybe they were undercover agents. Who knows, our waiter could have been one."

"That's a bunch of nonsense! That Eric is a chicken, that's all. He's just a chicken."

Should I pursue the subject? I wanted to find out what was going on. "I'm not afraid of any cops," I said. I waited for Paco's response. He just kept staring straight ahead. He didn't say anything. "What do we do now?" I wanted to know.

"I told Eric I would meet him at another restaurant. It's further on up the road. We'll try again."

"Should I get sick again?"

"I don't think so. If you had to, could you?"

"If you want me to do it again, I'll fake it all the way."

"Maybe I ought to get you in movies," Paco

smiled. "You're a great actress." We both laughed.
Paco showed a sense of humor sometimes. But I still
knew he was a very dangerous, violent man.

We drove to the other restaurant and went through
the same routine. We were seated at a table, and I ordered fried shrimp again.

About halfway through our meal, Paco leaned over
and whispered, "Here comes Eric." He nodded toward the door.

There stood a short, fat, ugly guy. "You mean over
by the door?" I asked.

"Yeah, that's him. That little, short guy."

Eric turned and walked into the bar. I said, "He's
not coming to us. Are you sure he knows we're here?"

"That was the plan. You're supposed to meet him
in the bar."

"What do you mean, meet him in the bar," I said.
"Is this going to be a drug deal, or a trick?"

Paco said, "All right, finish your shrimp, go to the
bar, and kind of make it with Eric. Then he'll take
you out to his car. He's going to give you something.
After he gives it to you, go to my car, and wait for me.
Got it?"

"Supposing he doesn't give me anything?" I asked.
"Then what?"

Paco clenched his fist. "Eric is smarter than that.
He'll give you something. And whatever you do, sit
there and wait for me. Do you understand that?"

Now I knew what was happening. Eric was probably going to give me some drugs. I was about to become a drug courier.

I quickly finished my shrimp. I was too nervous to enjoy them. I wiped my mouth and stood up.

Just as I did, Paco whispered, "Pretend you're soliciting him, and don't act suspicious." I nodded and walked off.

The bar was dimly lit. My eyes tried to get used to the darkness. I saw a couple of guys look at me. Their eyes went up and down my body. I knew both of those guys had money. Too bad I wasn't there to turn a couple of tricks, I thought to myself.

Then I saw Eric. Our eyes met, and I smiled. He didn't smile back. He looked kind of mean.

I walked over and sat down next to him. How should I handle this? Then I rememberd what Paco had said. Set him up just as I would set up a trick.

The bartender came over. "What'll you have," he asked. I looked up at him. I was too young to drink.

"I'll have a Coke," I told him.

"A Coke? That's all you want?"

"Yeah, I'm just getting over a severe drinking habit," I said sarcastically.

The bartender laughed. So far, so good, I thought. I reached down and put my hand on Eric's leg. I began to rub it. He looked at me and smiled. Then he put his hand on my leg and began to rub. I sure hoped Paco knew what he was talking about. This guy was responding awfully fast. "Want to go out?" I asked him.

"Beg your pardon, miss?"

"Want to go out, you know, go out?" I repeated, a little louder. I had thought the guy would say yes right away. Paco had better know what he was talking about!

He smiled. Then I felt a hand on my shoulder. I looked up. There stood a big, tall guy. He said, "Young lady, I don't think your presence is wanted in our establishment."

My heart sank. Things were going wrong. What would Paco do if I blew this? "Wh-what did you say?" I stammered.

"Young lady, I was standing just a couple of feet away from you. I heard you solicit this customer of ours. Now get out of here, before I call the cops!" I'd been caught red-handed. Paco was going to be furious with me.

Then the guy I'd been trying to pick up said, "Sir, I happen to be Detective Strassels of the L.A. Police Department. I was just north of here on a case, and thought I'd stop by for a quick drink. I'm off duty, but why don't I just handle this matter for you."

Now I was really scared. This guy was a cop! Was Paco going to get me arrested? Then I suddenly got angry. Paco had set me up.

The guy grabbed me by the arm and started marching me toward the door. "Hey, you don't have anything on me," I protested. "I was just trying to be friendly. Just asking for a date. I'm no prostitute. You can't get me for something like this!"

Most of the other guys in the bar were watching. One of them yelled, "Hey, mister, be easy on her. She's just a young kid."

154   KARI

"These little tramps should all be put in jail," my captor snarled back.

We walked through the restaurant section. I saw Paco at his table, watching us. I mouthed the words, "I got arrested." Paco turned and looked the other way, out toward the ocean. I couldn't believe it. Paco had really set me up.

Out in the parking lot, I made my last try. "Come on, officer. Just let me go. I didn't mean any harm, and I'm not what you think I am."

"Kari, you were great," the guy said. "That was beautiful, just beautiful."

I stopped and looked at him. "Are you Eric Armentani?"

He had a big smile on his face. "Yeah, you got the right one."

"What in the world happened in there, then?" I asked, pointing to the restaurant.

"Well, I told them I was a cop, right?"

I nodded. "Well, are you?" I demanded.

Eric laughed. "No, I'm not a cop."

"Then why did you do what you did? You scared me to death!"

"I'll tell you something. In case you didn't notice, I didn't have to pay for my drink. They thought I was a cop doing my duty, and I walked out without paying a dime. I ordered the most expensive drink in the house, too."

I didn't know whether to laugh or get mad. I finally said, "Well, Eric, at least I can be glad you didn't bust me."

"Come on over to my car," he said. "I've got something for you." When we got to his car, he reached under the front seat and pulled out a brown package. It was about half the size of a shoe box.

"Take this to Paco's car," Eric said as he handed it to me. Then he jumped in his own car and took off. I looked down at the package. I knew what was in it. Cocaine. I was probably carrying hundreds of thousands of dollars' worth. What would happen if the cops came looking for me now? If I got busted with this stuff, I would die of old age in prison. How stupid of me to be doing something like this.

I walked over to Paco's Rolls. I had to get into it, but I wondered if it was locked. Paco must have locked his car. Now what?

I tried the handle. The door opened. I sat down and locked the doors. I wondered why Paco didn't lock his Rolls Royce. That was really stupid. But then he probably had enough money to buy a Rolls Royce dealership, anyway. Material things didn't seem to matter to him—only drugs and prostitution and killing other pimps.

In a moment Paco came walking up. I reached over and unlocked the door.

The package was on my lap. When Paco saw it, he was furious. "Put that package under the seat," he snapped. "You're stupid, kid." I shoved the package under the front seat.

"Don't you know somebody could have seen you with that?" Paco went on. I felt like telling him that nobody knew what was inside of it except him, but it wasn't worth the hassle.

We pulled out of the parking lot and headed down the highway. I said, "Eric really scared the living daylights out of me. He pretended he was a cop to get me out of there."

"Eric does have a sense of humor, doesn't he?"

"He does, but it sure scared me. I thought maybe you had set me up to get busted."

Paco said, "Kari, you've got me all wrong. No way am I going to let you get busted. You're very valuable to me. You make a lot of money for me, in more ways than one."

I knew what that meant—out in the street as a prostitute, and now, as a drug carrier. I knew I was valuable as long as I suited Paco's purposes. I felt disgusted.

We drove back into downtown L.A. and pulled up in front of a big hotel. Paco said, "All right, I want you to take the package up to room eleven-oh-four. There you'll be given another package. Bring it to me."

"What's that room number again?" I asked.

I shouldn't have said that. Paco got mad. "Eleven-oh-four, not eleven-oh-five or eleven-oh-six. I said eleven-oh-four," he screamed.

"I just wanted to be sure," I said defensively.

Paco grabbed my arm. "I'll carve the number on your arm with my switchblade!"

"Don't do that, Paco." I jerked my arm back. "There'll be blood all over the place."

Paco reached into his coat pocket. "Here, I'll write it on your arm, then." He took out his ball-point pen and wrote 1104 on my arm. He dug deep. It hurt. I said, "Okay, okay, eleven-oh-four. I won't forget it."

I felt myself starting to cry. I just couldn't believe what I had gotten myself into—such violence and hatred, murder, prostitution, and drugs. There had to be a way out of all of this.

Paco must have seen my tears. "What's the matter with you, kid?" But I didn't want to tell him. I knew he wouldn't understand.

He reached under the front seat. "Here, put the package in this bag. It won't look so conspicuous."

It was a shopping bag from a store. I put the package inside, got out of the car, and walked into the hotel lobby.

I looked around for the elevator. Then I saw two cops standing right next to the elevator doors. They looked directly at me. I held my breath. Would they bust me now?

How was I going to handle the two policemen—especially if they wanted to look inside the bag? Maybe they wouldn't bother me. I started to step into the elevator. One of the cops grabbed my arm. Now I was done for!

I looked up at the policeman. He looked straight into my eyes. Maybe this was my opportunity to get out of this life of crime. I would just tell him that Paco was outside, and they would arrest him. But what about the cocaine? Paco would say he didn't know anything about it, and that would leave me holding the bag.

"Do you have your key?" the cop asked.

"A key? Why do you ask me that?" I didn't know what he was talking about. I'd better stall him until I could figure out what he meant. "Do I look like I should have a key?" I asked.

"Yeah," the cop replied. "It's regulations that your key is your pass to the other floors. Are you a registered guest here?"

Time to put on an act. I stamped my foot. "Hey, mister! Do you know who you're talking to?"

The officer stared at me. I pointed my finger right at his badge. "Do you know who you're talking to?" I repeated.

The officer smiled. "Well, I'm talking to a cute little girl. Why?"

"Don't you know who my dad is?" I persisted.

"No, I'm afraid we don't. There are lots of people in this hotel, and we can't possibly know them all."

"Well, if I were you, I'd walk over to the front desk and ask them who my dad is. He's the owner of Universal Studios!"

"Goodness me," the cop smirked. "I guess we should be more careful whom we stop, huh?"

Was this working? I said, "Well, I'm going up to room eleven-oh-four. I'm going to get my father and bring him down. And I'm going to get him to tell the owner of this hotel to fire you. You should have more sense than to stop me."

Was I pushing my luck too far? I'd better be careful

and not get too mouthy. If they arrested me and looked in the package, it would be all over.

The cop said, "Well, usually people tell us they're the mayor's daughter. At least you didn't tell us that."

It was working. I knew how to handle them now. "Listen, I was just kidding," I said apologetically. "Actually, my mom and dad and I flew in here from New York yesterday. Dad's a screenwriter, and he's trying to get a script accepted by Universal Studios. I don't even know who owns Universal Studios, to tell the truth."

The cop smiled. "I appreciate your honesty, kid. I knew you were telling us a story, anyway."

Just then the elevator door opened. I held my breath and stepped into it. The cops didn't do anything.

The elevator door closed. I pushed the button for the eleventh floor. That had been too close!

What awaited me in room 1104? Would everything turn out all right?

The elevator stopped at the eleventh floor. A sign said rooms 1101 to 1118 were down the hall to the right. I followed the signs to 1104.

I knocked on the door. There were footsteps and then a long pause. There was one of those little peep-holes in the door. I knew they were looking at me.

"Yeah, what do you want?" came a deep voice.

"I'm here to deliver a package."

"What kind of package are you delivering?"

"Why don't you open the door and find out?" I said.

There was some rattling at the lock. The door opened. The next thing I knew, a great, big, hairy arm reached out and grabbed me. It jerked me into the room. The door slammed.

I was looking up into the eyes of a huge guy. I glanced beyond him. There were two other guys, standing with their feet apart and their hands in their coat pockets. I knew they were hanging onto guns.

"Okay, what's your game?" the big guy growled.

"Does the name Paco sound familiar?" I asked.

"Yeah, we know Paco. And what do you have there?" I held out the bag. One of the other guys snatched it out of my hand and opened it up.

Then the big guy locked the door. I was trapped inside.

He pushed me toward the center of the room. One of the guys said, "Hey, Paco knows how to pick them. You're sure a cute little thing, aren't you?"

I didn't like the way he said that. Certainly he wouldn't take advantage of me. At least I hoped not. "I understand you have a package for me," I said hesitantly.

The big guy said, "Not so fast. Stay there for a minute." He took the package into the bathroom and shut the door. I'm sure he was in there seeing if it was really cocaine—or whatever it was. Or maybe it was a bomb. Would this be Paco's way of getting back at these guys? They certainly didn't look like three guys you could trust.

As I stood there, one of the guys came up and slipped his arm around me. I stepped away. He

grabbed me and turned me around to face him. "Give
me a kiss," he commanded. I looked up at his face.
He had a big scar on his cheek. And he was ugly—
and sick-looking.

"My father told me never to kiss a stranger," I told
him.

He threw both his arms around me and pulled me
close—real close. I could feel the pressure of his body.
"But your daddy didn't know all the fun you'd be
missing," he leered. "Pucker up, little girl. I want
you."

Paco hadn't warned me about this. What should I
do? I twisted my head back and forth. I wasn't about
to let those filthy lips touch mine.

He reached up and grabbed my hair. "Hold still."

With a quick thrust, I brought up my knee. It
caught him square between the legs. He screamed
and doubled over.

He reached in his pocket, and suddenly I was staring at a gun. "I ought to kill you, you little snot!" my
would-be rapist gasped.

Just then the bathroom door opened. "What's all
the yelling about?" It was the big guy again.

The guy I had kneed was pointing his finger at me.
"That little brat hurt me, man. She hurt me bad."

"Well, then keep your hands off her," the big guy
ordered.

He shut the bathroom door again. The other guy
started for me again. I said, "Mister, you heard what
he said. If you lay a hand on me, I'll kill you. You
understand?"

I was trying to act as tough as I could. My heart felt as though it were coming out of my chest, I was so afraid.

The guy took another step toward me. I looked at his partner, who had been watching the whole time. "Tell this friend of yours to keep his hands off me," I told him. "If he doesn't, I'm going to cut him."

He still kept coming. I reached in my blouse and flicked out my switchblade. "Look, man, I don't know who you are, but I think I should tell you who I am. I've been on the streets for quite some time, and I've handled them all—big burley guys, short guys. I've really cut them up. I'm the quickest knife on the streets. Ask any of the girls out there." I thrust the knife at him. "I dare you to step toward me," I challenged.

The guy put his gun back in his pocket. Then he walked over to the lounge and sat down. I stood there, my feet apart, ready to defend myself.

Finally, the big guy came out of the bathroom. He had a larger package with him. "Okay, everything's all right. Take this to Paco."

He held out the big package to me. Then he pulled it back. "Do you want to work for me?"

"What do you mean by that?" I asked.

"You work for Paco, don't you?" I looked the man up and down. "Yeah, I work for Paco. Is there anything the matter with that?"

"Paco's days are numbered. He's got lots of heat after him, man—lots of heat. Any day now, he's going to get busted."

If I played along, maybe I could get some information back to Paco. I said, "Yeah, he knows about it. In fact, he told me about it yesterday. I guess the heat is out to get him, huh?"

I was hoping his answer would tell me something, and I wasn't disappointed. "Yeah, the cops got his place in Beverly Hills staked out, and the apartment, too. I understand they're planning to bust him tomorrow night."

"He knows about it," I lied. "I guess he's paying off somebody in the narcotics squad, and they tipped him off. But after our deal here, he's catching an airplane and flying out tonight. I think he's going down to Acapulco."

"That's just what I meant," the guy said. "Paco's going to be gone with the money, but what about you?"

He had me. I had to think of something to say. "He's taking me with him," I told him.

"Listen, no matter where Paco goes, they're going to catch him. I bet you when he gets off that airplane in Acapulco, the Mexican police will be there. He's hot, I'm telling you. You had better dump him, quick, or they'll take you, too."

Was this guy lying? At any rate, I knew I could never work for him—absolutely not. I didn't trust him and especially the other guy working for him. He would have raped me for sure.

"I'll think about it, okay?" I said. I hoped that would get him off my back. I had to get the package out of there. And I had better warn Paco.

I started toward the door. He unlocked it and gave me the package. "Tell Paco, if he wants to make a big sale before he takes off, to let me know."

"Well, I'm sure that what's in here will tide him over," I replied.

"Listen, you don't understand. If they bust Paco, he's going to be in for a few years. If I were him, I'd do business now. Be sure to tell him to let me know if he needs to make a big sale." I didn't say anything. And I wanted to get out of there as quickly as I could.

It wasn't until I got to the elevator that I remembered the policemen. They were going to wonder why I was leaving again so fast. I needed an excuse, but I couldn't think of anything.

The elevator stopped at the fourth floor, and an older man got on. As soon as I looked at him, I had an idea.

"Mister, I'm looking for a father," I said. "Are you a father?"

The man smiled at me. "Yes, I'm a father. I have three children—two girls and a boy."

"Well, that's good. You see, my dad died of cancer last week, and my mom and I are in this hotel. All of a sudden I had an overwhelming feeling about my dad. I hope you don't think I'm crazy or anything, but do you mind if I hug you?"

He stared at me, not sure what to say. He was embarrassed.

My plan was going to work! I grabbed the man and hugged him tight. "Thanks, Dad," I told him. "I needed that."

When I looked up at the guy, he was as red as a beet. I'm sure he didn't know what was happening. But I did.

The elevator stopped at the lobby, and the man waited for me to get off. I grabbed his arm and said, "Here, Dad. Let's walk out of the elevator together."

We stepped out of the elevator. There stood the two cops, both watching us. I said, "Dad, say hello to the two policemen."

The guy kind of stammered, "H-hello, gentlemen."

We walked right on by them. My little scheme had worked perfectly.

We headed toward the door. I said, "Mister, you saved my life."

"What?" he asked. "What did you say?"

"I was on my way to commit suicide," I said. "My father's death really shook me up. But I think I'll be okay now. I don't want to die. You helped me change my mind."

This time it was the guy who grabbed me. He threw his arms around me and hugged me tight. He said, "Young lady, don't ever think about that again. There is too much in life to live for." I hugged him back. At that moment, I really missed my dad. This man's children sure were lucky to have him for a father. The guy seemed to be so nice.

I let go and started to walk toward the front door again. He said, "Young lady, don't forget what I said."

We walked through the door together. There sat Paco in the Rolls Royce. I knew I was going to look stupid walking over to that car.

I looked at the man. I didn't want to disappoint him. "My brother is a big movie star," I told him, "and he's going to take me out for a bite to eat. Thanks for your help, mister."

As I stepped into the Rolls, the man watched from the curb. I didn't want to hurt his feelings, even though I was probably the biggest liar in Los Angeles.

Paco reached over and snatched the package from me. "What took you so long?"

"What do you mean, what took me so long? I thought I was pretty fast."

"Listen, all you had to do was deliver the package, get the money, and come down. And I saw you hugging that guy. You didn't try to turn a trick, did you?"

Would Paco believe my story? I'd tell him anyway. "Listen, Paco, it wasn't all that easy. One of those creeps up there tried to rape me. First, he wanted a little kiss. The guy was out of his head. I knew he wanted me on that couch."

"Well, you should have charged him for it," Paco snapped. "That's what you should have done."

That wasn't the response I wanted. "Well, I pulled my switchblade on the guy," I said. "I would've stabbed him if he had tried anything."

"But what took you so long?" Paco demanded again.

"Well, the big guy went into the bathroom and opened the package there. He was in there quite a while."

"All right, open the package while we drive. But

keep it down on the floor when you open it. I want to see what you have in there."

I put the package on the floor and started ripping it open. There was a box inside. I lifted off the top of the box. I stared in it. There were one-hundred-dollar bills stacked in there.

Paco was watching. "Reach all the way to the bottom," he said. "I want to make sure it's money all the way down."

He was the boss. I shrugged and started digging through the bills. My hand finally hit the bottom of the box. I picked up a handful of bills and brought it out. I looked at it. They were thousand-dollar bills! I couldn't believe it. I had never seen so much hard cash in all my life.

Paco said, "Okay, I'm satisfied."

"Paco, those guys back there seemed to be quite concerned about you," I told him. "They claim the heat is onto you. They said the cops are checking out your place. Not just the mansion, but the apartment, too. They claim you're going to get busted."

"Listen, Kari, in this business you're always going to get busted. I'll find a way out."

"I told the guys you'd be taking the money and flying to Acapulco," I went on. "I wanted to go along with them and see what kind of information I could get out of them. That's when they told me that the cops were going to nab you tomorrow night."

"Kari, you hear all kinds of rumors in this business. You learn to discount them and just do your thing. I'm not afraid of anybody. I'm not afraid of the cops.

I'm not afraid of pimps. I'm not even afraid of those guys back there at that hotel. All I do is make my money and mind my own business."

Paco certainly wasn't afraid. But suppose what those guys had said was true? I did not want to be around Paco when he got busted.

"They also said they would buy more dope if you wanted to sell," I went on. "They look like they have lots of money. They told me to tell you that."

I waited for Paco's answer. Did Paco have lots of dope? How rich was he, really?

"How much would they buy?" he wanted to know.

"I don't know. I told them you were going to Acapulco, and they wanted me to tell you that you should sell your dope now, before you go down there."

Paco reached over and grabbed me. "How much did you tell them?"

"I didn't tell them anything, Paco. I made up a story about your going to Mexico. I was just trying to get information from those guys. Enough information to save you from getting busted. That's what I was trying to do."

"Listen, Kari. In this business you don't tell anybody anything. You only tell them enough to get your money. Then you get out. And you get out quick."

Paco was getting mad. I said, "I was only trying to help. Just trying to help."

"Well, your trying to help can get us into trouble. Next time you don't say one word. You hear me?"

I nodded. I didn't want Paco getting furious. He could easily kill me.

Paco stopped the car and went around to the trunk. He came back with some bags. I looked at them. They were bank deposit bags. There were five of them—for five different banks.

We were on a deserted street. Paco put the money in the bags with deposit slips. So that's what he did with his money. He deposited it in all those banks.

We drove to the five different banks. Paco put the bags in the night depositories. That was very clever.

Then Paco stopped and used a pay phone. Who was he calling now?

This time, it was a calm conversation. When he got back to the car, he said, "Those guys want to buy a hundred thousand worth of dope."

"What guys?" I asked.

"Those guys back at the hotel. I have some dope to sell, and I called them."

I didn't want to go back to that room again—especially with that one guy. I said, "Paco, the one guy really got rude with me. If I go back there now, I don't know what's going to happen."

"Well, you don't need to worry about that. You don't trust anybody in this business. I've made arrangements not to go back there, but to another place. We're going to go down to Long Beach. That's quite a ways away, but I can't trust anybody. That's how you survive."

We drove to another part of the city. I didn't recognize it. Paco went into an office building. There was a night guard who let him in. I thought, that was strange.

A little later, Paco came out with another package.
This was an office building. I wondered where Paco
had picked up the dope. But I was convinced he had.
Maybe there were some foreign trading businesses
here. I knew a lot of cocaine came from Colombia.
Maybe this was a front for a Colombian operation.

Paco got into the car. "Everything okay?" I asked.

Paco nodded. "Yeah, everything is fine."

"Do you mind if I ask you where we're going to
meet these guys?"

"We're going to meet them down by the dock for
the boat to Catalina Island, at the open pier."

"Do you trust those guys?"

"No, I don't trust those guys. They're trying to
muscle their way in on my connections in Colombia.
If you turn your back to them, they'll shoot you."

"Then why are we meeting them in a deserted
place like the docks at Long Beach?" I wanted to
know.

"I'm armed. And here, I want you to take this."
Paco reached under the front seat. He handed me a
gun, a small one.

"What am I going to do with this?" I demanded.

"You're going to use it, dummy. If they try anything, pull the trigger. It's loaded."

"But, Paco, where am I going to put it?"

"You put it in your blouse; that's where you put it.
Same place you put your switchblade."

It was almost too big for that. I said, "Are you sure
that's where I'm supposed to carry it?"

"Stuff it in. You'll be all right."

I opened my blouse and pushed in the gun. It was cold. And it was scaring me to death. Suppose it went off while it was in there. I could imagine what would happen.

Paco said, "Don't be afraid to use the gun, Kari. It's either you or them. If something goes wrong, they'll kill you. Kill them first."

We finally got down to Long Beach. We drove out toward the dock where the Catalina ferry departs. The closer we got, the more scared I got.

I just knew something would go wrong, terribly wrong. And I was soon to find out what.

12

Paco and I sat there, waiting. "Do you think those guys will be coming?" I finally asked.

"Yeah, they'll come. They're too greedy not to."

Well, I didn't like those guys. In fact, I didn't like anybody in this business. And I had an inner fear that something was going to go wrong tonight.

Paco kept glancing this way and that. "I smell a cop," he said suddenly. I almost leaped out of my seat.

"Where?"

"There's nobody in sight," Paco answered, "but I have a feeling there's a cop around here somewhere. Stay here. I want to look around."

He got out and closed the door. I peered through my window. There was absolutely nobody around, and it was very late at night. How could Paco know a cop was here?

Paco walked out toward the dock. Then he turned and walked around the building. I saw him pull on a couple of doors to see if they were unlocked. Everything was locked and secure.

Maybe I had better look. I stepped out of the car. I looked one way and then the other. There was nothing. I started to walk away from the car. Paco saw me. "Kari, get back in that car!"

He must have seen something. I ran back to the car, jumped in, and locked the door.

Paco was still looking back and forth. Then he walked over to the car.

I unlocked the door, and he jumped in. "Don't you know what you just did?" he demanded.

"Listen, I was just trying to help you out. If there's a cop around, I want to find him, too. I don't want to go to jail."

Paco interrupted. "You left my bundle of cocaine sitting here in the car, all by itself! Wherever you go, the cocaine goes, understand?"

"You mean I should have picked it up and taken it with me out there?"

Paco slapped me across the face. It stung. "Don't be stupid, Kari!"

That made me mad. But I didn't dare complain. I knew Paco was nervous, and he was capable of just about anything right now.

But why did the cocaine have to go with me? And then it hit me. I was Paco's carrier. If we got busted, he'd blame me. If the cops caught me with the cocaine, I'd be getting the rap. I was going to have to be very careful. No way were they going to catch me with a package of cocaine in my hands.

Paco and I saw the car at the same time. "Hope it isn't the cops," he said.

My stomach turned over. What would I do if it was the cops?

Paco said, "Okay, Kari. Walk over to that building and stand there. But keep the coke behind your back. Kind of lean against the wall."

Sure enough, it was exactly what I had thought. Paco was going to get me busted with the cocaine.

"Why don't you walk over there," I told him.

"I give the orders around here," Paco screamed at me. "Now get out of the car before I do you in!"

I looked down at the package on the floor. If I got busted with it, they'd lock me up and throw away the key for sure. "But what if it's the cops?" I persisted.

"Kari, you do what I say. Now get out of the car. And if you try anything funny, I'll kill you."

Paco was approaching the danger point. I had no choice. I got out of the car with the package and walked toward the building. I looked at the car approaching. I still couldn't see beyond those headlights. If it was the cops, I was going to throw the package and run for it. I would worry about Paco later.

The car got closer. And then I saw clearly. It was not the cops. I breathed a sigh of relief and started walking toward it.

Paco was looking at the car, too. Then he caught sight of me. "Back against the wall, stupid," he hollered.

What was going on around here. If it was our buyers, why get so upset?

"It might be the cops in a different kind of car," Paco yelled to me.

A wave of resentment washed over me. The gall of Paco to treat me like this. I was a slave. And he demanded anything from me. How had I ever gotten into this mess?

The car drove by Paco. There were four guys in it, and they stared at me. Then I recognized the guy sitting next to the driver. It was the big guy from the hotel.

The car went about fifty feet farther and stopped. All four guys got out. They stood there, looking at Paco and me.

Paco started to walk toward their car. "Stay right where you are, Paco," the big guy called.

Paco reached for his pocket. I knew that was where he kept his gun. "What's up, Bruno?" he yelled.

"I don't trust you, Paco," came the answer. "You stay there, and I'll stay here. That's how we'll do this deal."

Paco said, "Hey, Bruno, don't get so nervous, man. Everything is going to be cool. I don't understand. What's bugging you?"

"I just want to be safe," Bruno yelled back.

This dialogue was certainly crazy. I had never heard anything like it.

"Okay, I've got what you want," Paco said, "and you know the price."

"All right, Paco. Don't try anything funny," Bruno replied.

So help me, I couldn't figure this out. Why was

everybody being so mysterious all of a sudden? I thought this was just an ordinary drug transaction.

"Okay, give me your package," Bruno demanded.

Paco motioned for me to head toward Bruno. Now I really was scared. Something was drastically wrong about this whole transaction.

I started toward Bruno. "Is she armed?" he yelled to Paco. I stopped, waiting for Paco's answer. What should I do?

One of Bruno's thugs started toward me. "What do I do?" I hissed to Paco.

Paco stood there, staring at me. I looked back at Bruno. Then I looked at the guy coming toward me.

Bruno yelled again, "Does she have an iron on her?"

I knew I had a gun—and a switchblade. What should I say?

By now the guy was right next to me. "Hey, good-looking," he said nastily. I looked up at him.

Sure enough. It was the guy who had tried to force himself on me before. He wasn't going to try anything now, was he?

"Come here, Kari," Paco commanded. I started to go over to him.

"Both of you, don't move!" Bruno shouted.

I stopped in my tracks. I was caught between two violent men. If Paco yelled at me to pull my gun, I knew it would be the most difficult choice I had ever made. If I obeyed, Bruno's thug would probably shoot me. If I disobeyed, Paco would probably kill me, anyway. I could feel my knees shaking.

"Paco, what do you want me to do?" I asked.

"Just stand there and do nothing. I am not letting this guy Bruno pull one on me."

Then I heard Bruno yell in back of me. "Andrae, search her!"

Andrae came up to me and immediately reached in my blouse and jerked out the gun. As he did, the end of it scraped against my body. I almost cried out from the pain.

"Look at what I got here, Bruno. A nice, little handgun. It's loaded, too!"

Bruno began to scream and swear. "Check her again," he raged.

Andrae reached his big, filthy hands into my blouse again. He found my switchblade and pulled on it.

Andrae started laughing. "Shall I check her some more?" There was nothing more to check. I knew what he was thinking.

"Don't you dare touch me like that again," I told him, but it was too late. He grabbed me and started to move his hands all over my body. I wanted to kick him and scratch his eyes out. But I knew I couldn't. He had my gun and switchblade, and there was no telling what he would do if I resisted.

Andrae laughed some more—a dirty, filthy laugh. It was disgusting. He finally yelled, "Okay, Bruno. She's clean now!"

I felt so humiliated and embarrassed. I stood there, looking at Paco, and he stared back at me. I felt like bursting out crying, but I knew one thing. He didn't care.

"Come on, Paco. You're smarter than that," Bruno said. "How dare you to send an armed girl to me. I suppose you instructed her to shoot us all. Didn't you?"

Paco didn't say a word, so I yelled, "Bruno, that's not the truth! I do a number of things for Paco, and I find the gun and switchblade important. Understand what I'm trying to say?" I wanted to sound tough, but my voice began to quiver.

Paco started walking toward me. He said, "All right, you guys, the deal is off. It's off."

Bruno started moving toward me at the same time. Something drastic was going to happen. I started to back up.

The guy who had my gun pointed it at Paco. And then it happened! Shots rang out.

I saw Paco grab his chest. More shots rang out. I started running for it, still holding the package in my hand. But then I heard more shots.

Two bullets hit the pavement close behind me. I couldn't believe it. They were shooting at me!

There was a fence ahead. I clambered up it. Just when I got to the top, something hit me. Excruciating pain shot through my leg, and I fell over the fence. That's when I heard the sirens.

Bruno was screaming in the background, "Come on, come on! We've got to get out of here!"

Paco was right. The cops were around. I saw the flashing red lights approaching.

I still had the package of cocaine in my hand. I certainly didn't want to get busted with that. The ocean was close by. I heaved the package as far as I could. It splashed out there somewhere.

Police cars were coming from every direction. Now I was going to get it.

They surrounded everybody. I saw Bruno and the other three guys throw up their hands. The cops went over and handcuffed them.

Lying flat on the ground, I could feel a throbbing in my leg. I looked down at it. Blood was spurting out. I grabbed my leg and squeezed it tight. But it didn't seem to help much.

Then I saw two cops heading toward me, their guns leveled.

One of the cops said, "I saw her run this way." I tried to squeeze down as much as I could, but it didn't matter. They were soon on me.

One of them said, "Okay, young lady. Don't try anything foolish."

"I had absolutely nothing to do with this," I told him. "I was just an innocent bystander."

He reached down and picked me up. "Why, you're just a young kid! What's your name?"

I was too scared to give an alias. I just blurted out, "Kari Allensworth."

"Kari, you will have to come with us."

"Sir, look at my leg," I said. "I was shot."

The cop bent over and looked at my leg. "You're lucky to be alive," he told me. "You could have been shot in the head."

I knew he was right. But what was he going to do now. Would I go to jail?

He took me over to the police car. The other officer went ahead and pulled a first aid kit out of the trunk. They started bandaging my leg.

"We'll take you to an emergency room," one of them said, "but first let me read you your rights." He went on to say that I could refuse to say a word, and the whole spiel. I didn't really pay much attention.

I looked back where Paco was. He was still lying on the ground. Nobody was tending to him.

"My friend over there." I pointed my finger. "Is he all right?"

"Is that your friend?" the cop asked.

"Yes, that's Paco," I told him.

"Of course that's Paco. All of us know Paco. Big-time drug dealer, big-time pimp. And you call him your friend?"

I'd better watch out. I didn't want to be implicated in this deal. I said, "Well, I just met him tonight, that's all."

The cop said, "Young lady, you won't need to worry about him."

He didn't know Paco. You always had to worry about Paco. Paco would get me, no matter where I went. "Why do you say that?" I asked.

"He's dead." I looked at Paco. Then I looked up at the cop again.

"Are you sure?" I asked.

"I know when a person is dead. In fact, I checked him personally. The guy got it five times. He was rid-dled, I mean riddled, with bullets."

I was stunned. I didn't know whether to be happy

or sad. I thought about it. Then I felt a sense of relief. At least I didn't have Paco to worry about anymore.

The cop slapped some handcuffs on me. "I'm not taking off," I protested.

"Just a procedure. Since your leg is shot up, we'll have to take you to the hospital."

Other police cars began to arrive. So far they hadn't asked about the drugs. I was hoping that by now the cocaine had sunk or had floated out to sea.

The two cops took me to the emergency room in a nearby hospital.

Fortunately for me, the wound in my leg wasn't all that bad. But I was hoping they would hospitalize me, and maybe I could escape. I had no such luck.

They took me to the police station, and I had to go through the horrible experience of being photo- graphed and fingerprinted.

And then they put me in a holding cell. There were other girls from the street there. I recognized a couple of them.

One of the girls said, "You really must've got hold of a tough john, huh?"

"I was with Paco," I told her. "He got murdered by a drug buyer."

A couple of girls gasped. "You mean Paco was your old man?" the first girl asked.

I nodded. I was glad to be rid of him, too. But now I had another problem. How many years would I have to spend in the penitentiary?

A little later I was led out of the cell and taken to a small room. There was a crowd of people there, and they started asking all kinds of questions.

I tried my best to lie out of all of them. I never would admit about the package of cocaine.

Finally they were through. One of the cops said, "Well, young lady, we really got what we wanted. Paco's dead, and we got the killers. We're still looking for their dope, but they'll be out of circulation for a while."

"That's kind of brutal, don't you think?" I asked.

"Young lady, in this business, everything is brutal. Drugs are a billion-dollar business, and people are getting murdered left and right. You ought to thank God that you're still alive."

I wondered about that. Was I better off alive than dead?

The cop continued. "We are going to release you now."

I stared at him. "You mean I'm not going to jail?"

"Well, we could hold you on suspicion, but there's no evidence. We found nothing on you."

I couldn't believe it! I was getting off scot-free. I stood up. I felt my leg begin to throb. "Can I just walk out right now?" I asked.

The officer nodded. "Yes, you can go. But if I were you, I would heed this advice. Get out of this town. Period. You've been involved with a guy like Paco, and he's dead. But if I know you girls, you'll get involved with another pimp. It's a vicious circle. Girls that mess around with pimps have a way of turning up dead."

I put a hand on the doorknob. Was this a trap? I

started to pull open the door. I turned and looked at the cops. There were six of them staring back at me. "Thank you, gentlemen. You have been kind to me," I told them.

No one answered. I smiled, but they didn't smile back. Then I opened the door and stepped out. I walked down the hall and out the front door. I stood in the street. I was free! At least for the moment.

13

I limped down the street. The bullet wound in my leg was throbbing.

Where should I go? I wondered. *Who would take me in?* The answer was, no one.

There was the money problem, too. I was flat broke. I knew where I had to go—the Sunset Strip. I stepped out into the street and stuck out my thumb. Three cars passed me, then one stopped.

"Where you going?" the driver asked after I had jumped in.

When I told him, he giggled. I slid over next to him. I had to have money.

Before we got to the Strip, I took the guy to my usual place. He gave me fifty dollars.

I went back to the street and started to hustle. My bandaged leg didn't seem to matter. I had no pimp now, so the money was all mine.

It was late. I bought some dope and got off. Then I went to a hotel and rented a room. I slept, exhausted.

The following night I was back on the street. I had

gotten a few tricks and was looking for another when a woman walked up to me. She smiled. I looked at her. Who could this be?

In her hand was a book. "My name is Marilyn Osgood," she told me. "Here is something you might want to read."

She pushed the book at me. Oh, no, she had to be from some cult—probably a bunch of weirdos.

But I looked at the cover. It was a picture of an attractive-looking girl. I looked at the title of the book. It was *Patti*.

I looked at the woman. "How come you're giving this to me?" I demanded.

"It's the story of a girl who used to work on the streets in New York. It's very interesting reading, and it might help you."

What did that mean? I looked at the woman, and she smiled back at me. "I guess you don't understand, lady. I don't need something like this," I told her.

"You probably don't think so now. But why don't you just put it in your purse, and maybe when you have a chance, you can read it."

If it would help get rid of this lady, I might as well agree. I said, "Oh, thank you very much, ma'am. I'll sure read it. In fact, I have a little spare time every now and then."

She smiled again. "And God bless you, young lady. What is your name, so that I can pray for you?"

The lady wouldn't give up. But I decided to go along with her. "Kari Allensworth," I said.

"Well, Kari, our church will pray for you. We have a ministry out here in the streets for girls like you. I believe that God will change your life."

"Ma'am, I'll take the book, and I appreciate your prayers," I said, "but I am kind of busy now. Okay?"

"I certainly do understand, honey," she told me. "Thanks so much for the privilege of meeting you. And I know that you are going to enjoy the book."

The woman started backing up. That was better. I turned and walked the other way.

Halfway down the block, I looked back, hoping she wasn't going to follow me. She didn't.

I got a few more johns that night. Then I bought my dope and got off.

I went back to my hotel room.

Lying on my bed, I thought about my life. Then I remembered the book. I got up and went over to my purse. I opened the book and began to read.

The more I read, the more I saw my own life. Patti was a girl like me—a runaway. She had gone to New York City and became involved with a pimp.

I couldn't put the book down; the story was so fascinating. I read all the way to the end. At the last few pages, something grabbed me.

Soon I found myself weeping. I knew I had been wrong, terribly wrong. I knew I was fortunate to be alive.

Then, in the book, Patti was asking me if I would like to receive Christ as my personal Saviour.

I had never heard of that before. She told me that

all I had to do was acknowledge that I was a sinner and ask Jesus to forgive me, and then, by faith, receive Him in my heart.

In that hotel room, I found myself weeping and crying. And I was saying the prayer that Patti had asked me to pray.

After I invited Jesus into my heart, something drastic happened. I felt a weight lift off my shoulders. Something had changed.

The last page of the book told about the Walter Hoving Home in New York. I wondered if they could help me. Was this place for real?

I saw the picture of the Walter Hoving Home. It was beautiful. But did it really exist? I felt so good about my experience with Christ, maybe something had really changed. Or maybe I was losing my mind. I had to find out. I called the number.

A girl answered. "Is this place for real?" I asked her.

She chuckled. "Yes, we are for real."

Then I told her about reading the book *Patti.* I suddenly found myself pouring out all my problems.

The girl on the phone was named Debbie. She said she worked at the Walter Hoving Home. She said, "Kari, why don't you come here for help. That is why we are here."

It seemed almost like a dream. Could this be happening to me?

I told Debbie about reading the end of the book. Debbie told me that really happens. Many people read the book and receive Christ.

"Why don't you come to the Walter Hoving Home," Debbie said again. "We have a wonderful home, and Christ wants to teach you how to really live." Before I could answer, she said, "Let me pray for you right now."

As Debbie prayed, I began to cry again. I couldn't believe I had gotten so far into sin—the pimps, the tricks, the drugs, and all the rest. I desperately needed help.

And Debbie's prayer was so peaceful and soothing. She finally said amen.

"I appreciate talking to you," I told her.

Debbie said, "Kari, in just a moment we will say our final good-byes, but why don't you get on an airplane tomorrow morning and come to New York. You will never be sorry for that decision."

I thought about it. This was my chance to get out. I had no pimp at least for the moment. And the cops weren't going to prosecute me. This would be the perfect time.

"You mean I can come just like I am, tomorrow?" I asked.

Debbie began to explain to me what I was to do. It didn't seem to be so terribly hard. She told me how to get from the airport to the Walter Hoving Home. I knew I had enough money for the trip. I decided to do it.

And I did come to the Walter Hoving Home.

I am here now. I just can't believe this place. God has provided such a wonderful setting. And there are more than sixty girls like me here, all learning how to really live in Christ.

Oh, yes, I have had my ups and downs. But I would much rather be here than out on the street. That life is forever behind me.

And what about you? You might be in the same terrible circumstances that I was in. If that woman hadn't given me the book *Patti*, I wouldn't be here at the Walter Hoving Home today, safe and secure.

But right where you are, you can know Christ in a wonderful way. He can lift the burden of sin off your shoulders.

You could be a prostitute, a drug addict, or you might be in jail. Or you might just be in a normal home, reading about me now. I discovered that all of us need to have Jesus Christ in our lives.

Why don't you invite Christ into your heart?

All you have to do is acknowledge that you are a sinner. You know that. I don't even have to tell you so. And then ask Jesus to forgive you of your sins. He will do that.

The third step is just a step of faith. By faith, receive Christ into your heart.

Now let me encourage you in the next step. Find a group of Christians you can associate with. Join a good, Bible-believing church. Or, if you are in jail, find other Christians who are in jail with you, or contact a good chaplain.

Or maybe you want to write or call the Walter Hoving Home like I did. There is someone there to help you.

My prayer is that you will discover in Christ the joy of living, the same way I did. No problem is too great for Him to solve. No case is hopeless. Christ wants to live in your life now. Invite Him in.

And I will be praying for you, too.

Garrison, NY   Pasadena, CA

Some good things are happening at The Walter Hoving Home.

Dramatic and beautiful changes have been taking place in the lives of many girls since the Home began in 1967. Ninety-four percent of the graduates who have come with problems such as narcotic addiction, alcoholism and prostitution have found release and happiness in a new way of living—with Christ. The continued success of this work is made possible through contributions from individuals who are concerned about helping a girl gain freedom from enslaving habits. Will you join with us in this work by sending a check?

The Walter Hoving Home
Box 94304
218 South Madison
Pasadena, California 91109
Phone (818) 405-0950

Your Gifts Are Tax Deductible